CELEBRITY WEREWOLF

Andrew Wallace

CELEBRITY WEREWOLF

Andrew Wallace

NEWCON
PRESS

NewCon Press
England

First published in the UK by NewCon Press
41 Wheatsheaf Road, Alconbury Weston, Cambs, PE28 4LF
April 2019

NCP 182 (limited edition hardback)
NCP 183 (softback)

10 9 8 7 6 5 4 3 2 1

ISBN:

978-1-910935-98-9 (hardback)
978-1-910935-99-6 (softback)

Cover concept and design by Ian Whates

Minor Editorial meddling by Ian Whates
Book layout by Storm Constantine

From The National (page two)
Saved... by a werewolf?

Sally Wisniewski (21) was jogging in a park in Kent when she was attacked by John Fonting (37), who had been stalking her for a year. Unemployed Fonting, who writes a conspiracy blog, punched Wisniewski twice in the face, knocking her to the ground.

Fonting was interrupted in his attempts to rip off Wisniewski's clothes by 'this massive grey thing that was like a gorilla, but taller and more pointy'. The creature hurled Fonting against a tree, causing very minor injuries that incapacitated him.

Ms Wisniewski takes up the story:

"I was terrified at first," she says. "The werewolf, because that is definitely what he was, is about seven feet tall with these massive hands and claws. I was too scared to move, so he handed me my top and said, 'You'll get cold if you don't put this on.'

"His voice was very deep and posh, as if he was a prince, and his eyes were sad and kind of lovely.

"I took my top and he said, 'You're the first person I've ever spoken to. Thank you.' Then he was gone."

Fonting, released on bail pending further enquiries, said:

"I'm probably not allowed to say this, but frankly I think immigration has got totally out of control if they're letting werewolves in. I mean, how's he going to get a job?"

Fire Group Manager Ellie Bastido
(BBC News three days later)

The tower block had been burning for nearly eight hours and we couldn't get to the upper floors. My team refused to quit, but they were getting dangerously tired. You'd think that after the Kensington fire back in 2017 this wouldn't happen again, but here we are.

Suddenly there were screams behind me. I turned to find what I can only describe as a wall of grey fur; then I looked up and saw this face. I knew I should be out of my mind with horror, but he was beautiful. Terrifying, but… just gorgeous.

A werewolf. It wasn't even night, let alone a full moon, and there he was.

'Can I do anything?' he said and I swear with that voice he could have been reading the news.

Sometimes, all you have to fall back on is your professionalism and I said, 'Do you obey the normal laws of life and physics?' and he said, 'No,' and I said, 'A hundred people are trapped on those upper floors. Can you get them without hurting yourself?' He said, 'My fur is like armour and I can hold my breath for a long time, so I'll pop in and see what I can do. Please could you extend your ladders as high as you can?'

You've seen what happened next: that strange figure with people in his arms leaping out of a burning building onto the ladder. Nobody died. He kept going back in and obviously there was no point trying to stop him.

I thought he'd died when I didn't see him again. Turns out he'd searched the whole place twice, then gone out the back way.

Next thing I knew, he had his own chat show.

Report W#1 by Officer F8
Security Service:
Clearance Level Four

Subject is male, bipedal, seven feet tall to the tips of his ears and covered in thick but soft grey fur. The fur does not conform to normal wolf standards in that there is no fluffy 'under-layer'.

The skin appears black, although it is hard to see because of the fur's density. The fur pattern follows the humanoid shape, with a discrete thickening around the backside and genital area so that neither organ is visible.

There is no tail or any evidence that there was one. The physique is wiry rather than bulky, although strength and speed are sufficiently disproportionate to suggest an unknown muscle structure.

The hands appear too large for the rest of the body, although they have opposable thumbs and the additional size could be useful for gripping.

[Note: when the subject's grip was exercised, no available mechanism could force release]

Despite their size, the hands are exceptionally elegant and agile,

9

like those of a surgeon or pianist. The feet are similarly well formed, although they have pads. The legs do not have a wolf's 'hocked' rear leg and instead follow the human arrangement e.g. the lower leg bends backwards from the knee.

Further analysis of bone structure was not possible because subject is impervious to both X-rays and MRI scans. What little could be ascertained was achieved by touch, which the subject did not resist. The structure seems analogous to a human's although the skeleton feels different, as if the bones are harder.

The hands and feet have retractable claws. As with the fur, these features are unlike any found on a human or known animal and appear, as far as testing will allow, to be indestructible. No samples were therefore taken, because cutting through either fur or claws proved impossible.

[Note: subject did not object to the attempted removal and was very apologetic about our failure to secure a sample]

The skin is not quite as tough, although in any perceived attack the fur rises slightly to become a shield able to withstand blows with knives, an iron bar, and bullets fired from a comprehensive selection of currently available firearms representing a range of calibres. The experimental laser weapon was also ineffective, because the fur diffuses heat.

Silver has no adverse effect on the subject; neither do crucifixes, holy water or copies of the Bible, Koran and Talmud in any quantity or combination. Attempts at exorcism piqued the subject's interest, but yielded no tangible effects.

Subject offered a blood sample by biting his own arm and inserting the syringe needle himself. The blood is red, but a darker tone than that of either a human or wolf. Analysis of the sample is ongoing; thus far there is no match between the subject and anything on the DNA database. What is more, while humans and wolves have around 84% of DNA in common, the subject has only 42%.

Subject's head is neither wolf nor human, but as perfect a blend as can be imagined. The ears stand upright, and are large but proportional. The snout is long and well developed; in no sense does it represent a 'half-breed' or anything 'monstrous'. Despite this jaw structure, the subject has no problem with speech and is exceptionally eloquent.

The teeth are very white and, despite the subject's friendly demeanour, unmistakably those of a canine predator. However, witnesses have spoken of the subject's extraordinary physical beauty and it is hard not to concur with these statements.

Subject's hearing, taste and sense of smell are so well-developed that they have the same accuracy and sensitivity as our highest specification sensors.

No dangerous microbes, spores, bacteria or other agents were found on the subject. However, given the subject's 'alien' nature, it may be that these factors are present but not recognised. Certainly the subject does not appear to possess the usual bacterial infrastructure for digesting food.

There is nothing in the subject's saliva to suggest that his condition is transferable by biting. Injection of subject's body fluids into test animals and human volunteers had no effect.

Subject was requested to bite a volunteer, upon which the volunteer gained prolonged orgasm and then passed out. There were no other responses over the test period and the volunteer recovered fully with no ill-effects or physical alterations.

The subject cooperated fully with all tests including questions. At no time did he manifest rage or violence, despite the intensity of the procedures.

He claims to have no recollection of what he is, where he came from or why he is here. He 'became aware' about three weeks previously in a field near Wadhurst in Kent. This 'awareness' includes consciousness, language (including his name: 'Gig Danvers') and knowledge he describes as 'there if he needs it'.

He has spent the intervening time exploring the countryside. He only made himself known when he came to the aid of a young woman being attacked by her stalker and, later, during the rescue of twenty-four families from the upper floors of a burning tower block in South London.

Subject retains 'werewolf' form regardless of Luna phases or the time of day.

However, see Sub-File Note W#1X
Level 1 Eyes Only
Urgent decision required

From Celebrity Werewolf:
The Biography of Gig Danvers
By Andrew Wallace

A lot of people thought he was a special effect.

Even after irrefutable evidence was presented of a genuine werewolf living in the Kingdom of England, people continued to believe that he was some innovative blend of motion capture and hologram, because that explanation was preferable to the reality.

Gradually, though, he was accepted as genuine, which is when the real trouble began.

It didn't help that for all his physical assets and charm, he was hopeless in interviews. Take this memorable excerpt, three months after Gig's arrival, from Good Morning with Tricia & Abdul:

TRICIA: Gig, some people are saying you are Satan…

GIG: Are they?

TRICIA: …and your presence means the Second Coming is upon us.

GIG: I see.

[PAUSE]

ABDUL: Is either of those assertions… true?

[PAUSE]

GIG: You know, I'm really not sure.

No one else would have got away with it. As things were, an economy in meltdown combined with a culture that for no other reason than the process of change already felt itself besieged, had blended to create a country united only in the hatred its many opposing factions felt towards each other.

Gig's arrival hadn't overturned accepted cultural norms so much as hastened their inevitable decline. It left little to believe in, other than a wolfman on a morning TV sofa making a hash of pretending he wasn't the Antichrist.

Would Satan be this awkward, though? Surely, the Devil would relish the chaos of England as this once-proud country inched its painful way further into the twenty-first century. Instead, Gig effortlessly gathered support simply by having no idea what he was talking about or what he was doing.

At least, that's how it seemed at first.

Gig Meets Becky

Without Becky, I might have remained little more than an entertainer, because there would have been no Products and thus no Orchard Industries. Without me, Becky's career would have ended: another victim of the US evangelical anti-knowledge movement that increased its global influence following victory in the Second Civil War. The US was one of the Kingdom of England's few remaining trade partners, which meant previously unthinkable compromises were now the norm. State-sponsored academic science was an early casualty, particularly icky subjects like Becky's world-leading transgenics research.

The Security Services introduced me to Becky when she was working out of Imperial College in London. It had taken a while to get to her; everyone wanted to meet me, and I wanted to meet everyone in return. Nonetheless, my handler, Mehmet, a small, muscular Turkish man in his thirties, had somehow managed to get us through the crowds to the heart of the campus.

Becky was sitting in a corridor with her back to the wall, reading a hefty report. Students and colleagues moved around her, clearly used to this sort of thing. Becky ignored the racket as we approached, squinting as if to shut out the noise so she could read just one more line before being interrupted. Finally, she looked up.

I could hear her heartbeat, and the husky sigh of her breath. She didn't wear perfume and the faint tang of her sweat smelled of tealeaves. She had a chunky fringe and thick, messy brown hair to her waist. Her smile showed a big proud overbite, and there was a stillness to her blue eyes that could have been calm but was probably something else. Indifferent freckles marked a face that seemed additionally battered, as if the physical and emotional upheavals of thirty-nine years without moisturising were not enough punishment on the flesh.

"Gig, is it?" she said.

Her voice was several fortunes above middle-class, but like her face seemed curiously worn. She had a calculated way of speaking, as she worked that accent for maximum clarity and nothing else.

"Well who else is he going to be?" Mehmet said.

"And you are?" Becky said.

"George Smith," Mehmet said.

I looked at him. He shook his head slightly.

"George... Smith," Becky said and oh, the genius of mockery in her voice! I liked Mehmet and felt sorry for him. "Do you think you could get these other..." She waved at the students watching us, "these... somewhere else? Thanks."

Mehmet obliged, clearly without knowing why. Becky has an almost hypnotic authority that comes from saying things in a way that makes you want to obey her, even though she's annoyed you.

As the corridor cleared, Becky stayed on the ground, legs tucked beside her, looking up at me. She wore a short denim skirt with a home-embroidered pattern around the hem. It had glittery fragments, although some had fallen out. Her tweed jacket looked like a man's, while her shirt was that of a female estate agent: functional, but with a couple of frills where it counted. Her trainers fitted, but were mismatched.

"Becky," she said, patting her chest. "Becky D'Olivera."

"Gig Danvers," I said, and felt silly because she already knew that.

Becky nodded, and I was relieved to be spared the scorn with which she had devastated Mehmet.

"Good name," she said.

"I've just always known it," I said.

She nodded, got up; her right knee clicked and she grinned at me, her face over a foot below mine. I grinned back, aware of how different my smile was with its unapologetic canines, its fangy rows.

Becky turned, slapped an access card against a panel by the door and strode in. I followed and we'd gone through three maze-like labs before I realised I'd left Mehmet behind. Becky disappeared through another door, and I saw we were now in a different building. People gazed at screens or looked into microscopes, but stopped and stared as I passed.

"Good morning," I said.

A couple waved, most just carried on staring and one woman said, "It's afternoon."

We arrived in a room that looked like the freeze-frame of an avalanche, except instead of snow it was equipment and information in various forms, some pre-digital. Becky slotted my file into an opening whose structural integrity looked unlikely and turned to me as the door closed behind us. She reached up and touched my chest –

A Quick Word About Waking,
If That's What It Was

I first became aware in a field. I was... like this. I had no memory of being anything or anyone else prior to that moment and still don't. I didn't need to touch my body or look down at it, because there was no separation of mind and physicality.

It was a sunny day in October. The sky was cool blue. There were no clouds and the high, deep view was terrifying, the way truly beautiful things are.

There was sound everywhere.

A barn owl had caught a mouse and I could still hear its shriek echo off the trees. I heard worms in the soil, moles digging; a fox crossing the bottom of the field. By that time of the year, the birds were a lot quieter, but there were a few rooks calling and I could hear the dimensions in each cry. Something munched the grass beside me: a roe deer, just a little thing, chomping away. It stopped, looked at me and then went on with what it was doing.

There was a soft wind with a sharp edge. This sunny day would be the last one for a while. Everything around me knew that, and worked to put winter measures in place. There was a frenzy to it: a sensuous desperation.

I love music; anything musical made by human hands I love, but there has never been anything to compare with the symphonic density of that first waking moment.

My body was full of power. I was calm though; lying still, the wind in my fur bringing smells of leaf and animal. I could feel the bumpy earth; the grass as I pressed it down. I must have been lying there for some time, because the grass was warm.

I stretched and all that latent energy jangled through me, like each huge muscle was laughing. For a moment, everything appeared to spin, as if every possibility was rushing in to be realised...

Love

By the time I met Becky people had touched me many times, but no one had the effect she did. It was as if all my inner forces gathered at that hand-shaped area of contact.

I don't wear clothes; I'm kept 'decent', as people say, through a combination of well-positioned fur and telescopic genitals. This arrangement made the resolution of whether I prefer wolves or humans/men or women obvious at once.

"Goodness," Becky said, stepping back.

"Hm," I said.

Becky licked her lips and swallowed, then undid her skirt, which dropped as she stepped out of it. She seemed undecided about keeping on the jacket and shirt, so I sniffed her hair, which was delicious, and then stroked it. Becky gasped; I extended my claws and began to comb out the tangles.

Becky's head nodded forward, as if pleasure had drained her. My claws danced through the thick brown hair, making Becky shudder with delight as they touched her scalp. She tried to remove her clothes, but the effort was half-hearted so I did it for her.

I licked her face, her breasts, her sex and she stumbled. I picked her up, but had no idea how to establish a suitable position, so I rested her on my shaft and held her. She pressed into my fur, wrapped herself around me and for a long time we stayed like that in the sighing afternoon.

From time to time she shuddered; her smell changed and vibrations of intense pleasure shot through me, ebbing into lovely aftershocks. I could feel her tears soak through my fur: warm and then cool. I followed the heat patterns around her body with my palms, fingers sinking into her soft skin.

When Becky passed out I put her on the floor, gathered up the clothes and lay them over her. I wasn't spent, but rested my head on her anyway because it felt so very good.

She woke up when it got cold, as if the blue sky outside had spread down into her, reaching her lips. I kissed them until they were warm, and she smiled.

"Are you hungry?" she asked. "Do you eat?"

"Yes," I said, although as I did the now-familiar pain went through my head. "So long as I don't eat anything that ever had a brain."

"Huh," Becky said with that still look again. "You could probably tuck into some of the people around here without too much cognitive dissonance."

I found somewhere to sit and Becky shared her lunch with me.

"So," she said, washing down falafel with grapefruit juice. "You're a beautiful seven-foot werewolf. Where do you see yourself in five years' time?"

"With you."

Becky stared at me. I sensed she was not often lost for words.

"You're so sure," she whispered.

"I'm sure about lots of things," I said. "I feel connected to the world in a way I don't think most people are. I can sense patterns; such as how I hear entire registers, or get a sense of an incident, a life even, from the scents in a single breath. With you, it's especially powerful, because I feel I already know you and will always know you. I can't explain why."

Her smile was strange.

"I feel the same," she said.

"Good."

"I'm very promiscuous, though."

I shrugged and she threw her arms around my chest, breathing hard as if she was trying to inhale me.

"And… have you considered a career?" she said, when she finally let go.

"I thought just general werewolfing."

"What does that entail?" Becky said. "Howling at the moon?"

Her eyes widened.

"What is it?" I asked.

"Your face," Becky said. "I don't think I've seen anyone look so sad."

"I've never had the urge to howl," I said. "Just the thought of it makes my heart ache."

Becky went to say something, then stopped.

"I'm the only one, aren't I?" I said. "Werewolf, that is."

"Yes," Becky said. "And there's no secret society of vampires, mermaids and goblins either. There's… just you."

"I have no pack," I said. "That's why I don't howl."

"Maybe not general werewolfing, then," Becky said.

"I sense you have an alternative career plan."

Becky smiled.

"I've analysed the few samples the Security Service managed to get from you," she said. "No one could make sense of them, but I have a gift for that sort of thing. I think we can develop new technologies, based on a perspective of organic chemistry we hadn't even considered until you appeared."

"Weapons?"

"No, not weapons; that hadn't occurred to me."

"I'm very glad," I said.

"I was thinking of medicines," Becky said. "Maybe renewable power sources…"

Something jolted through me.

"Yes!" I said. "That would make the most perfect sense. You see, because I have this connection to the world, I feel we're all under threat somehow; that there is something growing, something dark under the things we don't notice."

"Do you mean environmental degradation?" Becky said.

"Yes, that, but also…"

I looked out at the chilly sky.

"…how our existence relies on mutual arrangements we barely understand, which are being wilfully ripped apart."

"How?" Becky said. "And who is doing it?"

"I don't know," I said. "But your idea, of a… company? Something commercial, that we would have complete control over; we could use it to create ways of reconnecting that damage and keep everyone together."

"It would protect you, too," Becky said.

"How so?"

"The sad truth is that if you're different it helps to be very, very useful."

Gig at the Launch After-Party of Orchard Product
(Nine months after his appearance in Kent)

The party has been going on for a while; I can hear its vibrations through the lift as I travel up with Helen. She and Becky have spent the precious moments they are not working themselves into a twitching daze trying to get each other fired, as usual. There is no sense hoping they will ever get on; they are like matter and anti-matter, the irascible fuel that drives the newly-formed Orchard Industries as much as I do.

I can sense Helen's residual anger, although no one else would be able to. She gives little away, but then Orchard's Agent is suited to inscrutability. She is tall, thin and favours tailored skirt suits in the kind of bright colours that go well with black skin. Her hair is a glossy, shoulder length bob whose upkeep requires constant attention, while her mouth is very full-lipped: an embarrassment of sensuality in a face of calm watchfulness.

Helen's rare smiles reveal teeth that are a bit gappy, which makes her look more fun than she is. On the few occasions I have touched her she has not responded, giving the impression I'm touching a woman made of wood.

She appears to be constantly sizing you up; then, when you

think she's finished, sizing you up again. Her management style is a quiet sort of directness that takes a person's half-buried racial nonsense and reflects it back.

Under it all I sense her struggle with unattainable goals of perfection, even though she knows they're absurd and not what I, as her notional employer, want anyway. Pride is alien to both of us; me because I don't understand it, Helen because of some deep shame I can sense in the way her body heat moves and the acne rashes she hides with makeup.

The lift doors open onto a garden at the top of a skyscraper, with a great view over the city at night. The omnipresent heat haze enhances the perspective, blurring the dense collection of lights into a pattern that is mysterious and vaguely threatening.

We stride in, to applause. I love being around people and feel my shoulders go back, proud to be here, to be accepted. The sounds, tastes and smells of the room whirl around me: delicate food and crisp wines mingling with perfume as it works its way through clothes to blend with pheromones and excitement; the many notes of conversation in their fast-evolving patterns; laughter, cutlery, glass; the swish of movement and layers of red and gold light.

As Helen disappears into the crowd, I'm handed a glass of champagne and clink it against others as they're held up. I chat to the Minister of Energy, the Head of the Security Service, three movie stars and four CEOs. Outside, the night hangs over streets grown desperate; the roof garden high enough to attenuate the sirens for everyone here except me.

I pick up a strange scent.

"Have all the guests arrived?" I say.

"Yes," Helen says.

She talks to me via a speaker in my ear and I reply via an equally tiny receiver on the back of my front left canine.

"Is anyone here who shouldn't be?"

"No."

We are in almost constant touch; her incredible mind able to determine the right opportunity from an ever-expanding galaxy of requests, demands and accusations. Currently, we are fighting the assertion that I am 'from space' (exact location unknown): the advance guard of an invasion of large, hairy aliens, the rest of whom are less polite than I am. There may be some truth in the assertion, although no strange meteorological phenomena occurred on the date of my arrival and no eerie craft appeared in the skies over England or anywhere else.

"What's wrong?" Helen says.

"I can smell... death."

I follow the scent to a cascade of plants at the periphery of the room, where something white moves. I dart around the edge of the greenery to find a male figure in bandages. The smell of death comes from him.

"Are you all right?" I ask him.

"Yes, thank you," he says. "Like you, I am a supernatural being."

"The Invisible Man?" I say.

"No! The Mummy."

He certainly has an odour of the grave, but it's mixed with old trainers, perspiration from a male body very much alive and a brand of after-shave that's meant to render you irresistible to women.

I realise the problem.

"Are you sprinkled with cremated human remains?"

"Ha!" the Mummy says. "I knew you'd get it. I strive for authenticity, you see. It's what Gran would have wanted."

"Well," I say, "thank you for coming."

"I'm also a journalist," the Mummy says.

"Anything I've read?"

The Mummy hesitates and says, "I write for *The Guardian*.

My human name is Otis Pyke-Jones."

"He doesn't write for *The Guardian*," Helen says in my hidden earpiece. "He once wrote a letter about badgers to *The Guardian* and they published it. He's here because he maintains a well-regarded technical blog, which we can use to seed ideas about our Products."

"Working on anything good?" I say to Otis.

"Yes!" Otis says.

He hesitates again and I notice it's not just the granny dust that bothers me; it's his extreme tension.

"You know, I'm a big fan of yours, Gig."

"Thank you, Otis," I say, chuffed.

"So what I'm going to ask you isn't easy."

I feel sorry for him.

"I'm sure it can't be that bad," I say.

He nods, then shakes his head.

"Tell me," he says, "is it true that Orchard Product 1 is actually werewolf venom?"

"Werewolf... venom?" I say.

"What?" Helen says.

"That in fact instead of an antibiotic it's meant to turn people into werewolves?"

"No," I say. "We tested it very thoroughly. Many of the original antibiotics no longer work. A claim like yours would mean a lot of people get ill or die. Do you want that?"

"Do you want everyone to be a werewolf?" Otis says.

"Not at all. I like everyone as they are."

"Nonetheless," Otis says, 'there's a company that has got hold of some samples and is testing them."

"All samples are accounted for," I say.

"And yet one of the pharmaceutical firms claims that O1 is a risk."

"Which firm?"

"DPS."

"Isn't that run by a guy who has trolled five women to their deaths?" I say.

"Yes," Helen confirms, and her voice is strained, as if she's fighting the urge to vomit. "Gavin Dergs."

"Otis, DPS are clearly making this up," I say. "O1 is going to hit their profit margins hard. If you print your story, understand that Gavin Dergs is playing you."

To his credit, Otis looks almost as worried as I feel.

The party is less enjoyable after that.

From Celebrity Werewolf:
The Biography of Gig Danvers
By Andrew Wallace

Thanks to a campaign of disinformation by rival pharmaceutical company DPS, sales of the Orchard antibiotic were seriously reduced. Ordinarily, the fortunes of a pharma-tech start-up would be of little concern to the public. However, Orchard was and remains a committed tax-paying corporation, so the malicious and inaccurate 'werewolf venom' rumour cost the Kingdom of England billions in lost revenue. Indeed, it is likely that these revenues would have rendered unnecessary the controversial bridging loan from the Northern Republic and resulting political nightmare.

Lamentable though this situation was, it became insignificant beside the sheer volume of preventable deaths. It is impossible to know exactly how many people died because of basic and treatable infection. However, the World Health Organisation carried out a study based on known death rates using a ratio of population size to wealth, establishing a figure of two million deaths over a three-year period. Such was the rumour's pervasiveness that even Orchard's decision to give the antibiotic away made little difference.

DPS escaped censure because the 'werewolf venom' claim

was never directly linked to either the company or its elusive founder, Gavin Dergs. However, Dergs and his companies were associated with extremist political organisations such as Saxon Jihad, whose website claimed that the disinformation had the desired effect of 'purging us of the hated weak'.

It was later found that a DPS subsidiary was selling its own version of the Orchard antibiotic.

Wash Up

"Where else could the leak have come from," Helen shouted. "Gig himself?"

She and Becky were in a hired meeting suite overlooking that stub of the M4 as it heads out of West London. The suite was booked randomly at the last minute to avoid any chance of surveillance. Its corporate blandness emphasised discreet shades of calming green, which were having no effect.

Becky leaned back on her chair, with only the rear two legs still in contact with the floor. She wore her trademark tweed jacket with nothing underneath except a white sports bra that wasn't hers. Her short leather skirt used to be much longer, until she hacked half of it off with a scalpel. Meanwhile, her knee-length boots were tailor-made and cost more than hire of the suite for a year.

Helen stood with her back against the window, which overlooked traffic moving with dull inevitability along the flyover. It was a grey, overcast morning that alternated between too hot and too cold.

Helen, ever conscious of properly staging a scene, knew she presented herself as a dark figure whose expression was in shadow. She stood very still in her beautifully tailored red skirt suit, and allowed waves of rage to wash out from her as if carried by the fluctuating light of strange weather.

Becky twiddled her hair and sniffed a lock of it, to Helen's obvious disgust.

"You're in charge of buying advertising space and whatever else it is you do," Becky said. "Information management is supposed to be your department."

"Your 'lab', then," Helen said.

"Not possible," Becky said.

Helen laughed.

"You think because it's chaos no one can take advantage of it?"

"I do think that, yes," Becky said.

"You have no way of tracking information," Helen said.

The front two chair legs slammed to the floor; Becky got up and strutted over to Helen, looking up into her face with an expression of contempt held in check by pity.

"Your inability to understand is not my problem," Becky said.

Helen regarded Becky as if she were some distasteful organic process.

"The money we have made so far is from advertising and media," Helen said, "which means I pay your wages."

Becky dropped to her knees and kissed the toe of Helen's red patent leather shoe.

"Thank you," Becky whispered.

"Gerroff!" Helen yelled.

Becky scrambled away to avoid being kicked in the mouth, laughing as Helen shook with rage.

"Don't you care what this means?" Helen said. "People won't use the O1 Product because they think they'll turn into a werewolf."

Becky stopped laughing and sprang to her feet, white-faced.

"Of course I care!" she shouted. "Why do you think I developed the Product in the first place? Your precious corporate martyr complex is becoming a serious problem."

Helen turned and looked out of the window. Her hair was perfect, but she ran her hands over it anyway, smoothing every shining strand. Finally, she turned around again.

"Becky, if I am a martyr it's because I am fully aware that you just want Gig to yourself. You have always wanted him for yourself. You always will.

"I am very sorry that my... crude skills are needed to enable you to do what you need to do. You disparage my work, while my every waking moment is spent celebrating yours."

"You don't mean that," Becky said. "You like being apart."

Helen's eyes glistened.

"How can you be so clever and so wrong, Becky?" she whispered. "You think I want to be apart because I don't want to have sex with you? Because I don't want to watch you have sex with Gig? I don't like sex, Becky. You have enough for both of us."

"You almost had me there," Becky said. "Then, sure enough, out comes the Victorian morality."

"You're alone too, Becky. Just like me, just like Gig. That's why you cling to him so hard."

"Which self-help book did that come out of?"

"Can't rightly recall," Helen said, her voice soft.

"Listen," Becky said, "if you can manage to expand your mind just a nanometer, understand this: you think there is a leak of information. There isn't. It's something else. I don't know what and I can't explain it yet, but... Did Gig ever tell you about why he's doing all this?"

"He's seeing off some 'darkness'. Not very helpful."

"It is helpful. Oh, Helen, we work with a werewolf! And contrary to a thousand years of cultural expectation, he is a kind and decent individual. Clearly things have changed in ways we do not yet understand. If that werewolf says there is something more going on that we cannot yet see, I think it behoves us to give it some credence, don't you?"

"By 'not helpful' I mean there is no obvious course of action," Helen said.

"There is," Becky said. "It's that we keep on, and on, and on and we don't let anything stop us, not now; not ever."

Helen thought for a moment.

"If you and Gig are right," she said, "then this… situation with Product 1 is just the beginning. It might get worse."

"It will get worse."

"It could explain you and me," Helen said.

"How so?"

"We're in training for a much bigger fight."

"Christ," Becky said, "then we really are in trouble."

Fetch
(Two months before the launch of Product 4)

Orchard Industries began in a nineteenth century school building in East London. The school had survived two world wars, numerous good ideas about education from politicians who hate teachers and a government private partnership scheme that even Becky couldn't get her head around. We bought the building cheaply after an attempt to convert it into flats fell through, and while Orchard eventually moved to a large office block nearer town, Becky's research department stayed where it was, much to Helen's annoyance.

Of the two, Helen appears more scientific. She works in a huge communication centre that looks like a TV studio, full of whiteboards, charts and people glaring at monitors.

Becky is the opposite. Her lab is a tip and her staff a shambles no one else would employ. She loathes computers and writes everything in a code she makes up every other day and then deliberately forgets. Her operation is secure because no one else has any idea what she is doing. Fortunately, she is a genius; with a unique gift that enables her to determine the hitherto unimagined structures of my DNA.

Despite Helen's reservations, I enjoy the walk to Becky's lab. There are always new people to meet, and sure enough I'm surrounded by a crowd the moment I leave Orchard Tower. They want photos, or to touch me; sometimes they hold their children up, as if I'm meant to bless them. I usually put the kids on my shoulders.

"Nice doggy!" a three-year old girl says.

"Charlotte!" her mother says, reddening.

"Woof," I say and the little girl laughs.

A young man with long hair dyed grey asks if he can film himself with me, howling. There's a brief awkward silence.

"I... I don't howl," I say.

His face falls; he is embarrassed.

"It's just that wolves howl to communicate to the rest of the pack," I say, "and... Well, there's just me, so..."

He gestures to the smiling crowd.

"We're all here," he says.

"Of course you are," I say.

We get some pictures together anyway, with no howling.

Once the signing and photography is done, I set off for the lab to look at final test results for Product 4.

The route takes me through areas left behind in the city's constant reinvention of itself. There is a community of sorts, often vulnerably housed or living on the streets and sometimes ill. They know I don't carry money; instead, halfway between Orchard Tower and Becky's lab we have set up a shelter with decent food, hot showers and a doctor who goes in once a week. The doctor is Becky, although she prefers 'professor' because she thinks Doctor D'Olivera has too many Ds.

Today, ten people remain from the crowd outside Orchard Tower, along with six locals on their way to the shelter. It's a nice walk, despite the weather being way too hot for March.

"All right, Muttley?"

There are eight of them, all male, in the mouth of an alley filled with old white goods like broken teeth.

"Hair of the dog, eh?"

I've heard that one, and the one before.

"Are those your pikey friends, Dogboy, you mutant? Did they put a curse on you?"

They are bulky and overweight; nobody has an actual neck and they all look as if they're made of spam. One has a Saxon Jihad tattoo on his arm.

"I'm really not sure," I say.

"Hark at him! Who do you think you are?"

Saxon Jihad throws a stick.

"Fetch!"

As the stick bounces on the road, I turn to the people with me.

"Into the shelter, if you wouldn't mind," I say.

They hesitate.

"It will help me if you do," I tell them.

They go; I set off after the stick and the gang follows me.

"He's actually doing it! Go on, Fido!"

People at the shelter are pointing phone cameras at me.

Helen calls.

"Gig," she says my earpiece. "There is live online footage of you fetching sticks for Nazis."

"I don't want trouble for the people with me."

"It looks like you're running away."

I turn and look at the gang, who also register as a set of heat patterns and smells: curry, lager and... lemonade?

"Who had the lemonade?" I say.

The gang stops and I see they now hold baseball bats wrapped in barbed wire.

"We all had lager tops, you furry wanker!" one of them shouts.

I thought I had them there. I try to think of something else and then they're on me.

A pattern to the blows reveals my attackers have been trained. Worse: people run back towards us from the shelter and, unlike me, they are not protected by indestructible fur.

I snatch a bat, break it and hurl the man who swung it against the others, scattering them. They bounce off walls and come at me again.

The people from the shelter reach us.

"Be clever," I tell them, "otherwise they'll say we started it."

Two of the larger street guys wrestle Saxon Jihad to the floor and use scissors to cut off his clothes. Before Saxon Jihad can respond, one of the street guys unleashes the contents of a jar of wriggling black.

"My spider collection!" the other yells.

Saxon Jihad screams and runs away, his nutlike genitals awriggle with large arachnids.

A baseball bat nearly hits –

"Becky!" I shout, because she's in the middle of it as usual.

I snatch the bat to parry with. An attacker misses me and hits his associate, who staggers off, bleeding. Another goes white and I hear his heart stutter; he collapses as it starts again, more weakly this time. One disappears under a mound of people from the shelter and I hurl another into a large wheelie bin, from which his legs protrude and kick slowly, as if he is attempting to tread water upside down. The last three jump at me; I throw them in the air and as they fall I sling them up again.

"Nazi juggling," Helen says. "Very good."

The men stop screaming and become large, sweaty beanbags. When I let them go they stumble off, grey with motion sickness.

It feels like victory, until fuel-accelerated flames erupt from the shelter.

From Celebrity Werewolf:
The Biography of Gig Danvers
By Andrew Wallace

Saxon Jihad's infamous attack on the homeless shelter brought about a change in Gig's business approach. Until then, his operation had been London-centric; however, once the decision had been made to combine operations in one purpose-built environment, it made sense to look elsewhere.

The first of these facilities was Orchard City in the northwest.

Its position close to the border wall with the Northern Republic (formerly Scotland and United Ireland) was interpreted as an overture to reopening trade with Europe following the series of calamitous trade wars and embargoes that had crippled the British economy.

The Northern Republic had long since left the UK, joined the EU and adopted the euro. Scotland then used oil revenues to establish the most powerful and advanced renewable energy infrastructure in the world and extend it to Ireland. The Republic now exported energy to Europe, the Kingdom of England and the Welsh Protectorate.

Nationalists in England, backed by powerful corporate interests and the landed aristocracy who had lost valuable holdings (particularly in Scotland), began agitating for an invasion of the North to reclaim what they saw as rightfully theirs, even though all of them now lived abroad.

They found a champion in Gavin Dergs, whose newly established security firm DSS offered low rates for 'the protection from squatters, gypsies and the like' of long abandoned country estates and farmland grown unprofitable without European subsidies. In practice, this tactic meant that DSS used the empty land as a series of interconnected training barracks for what pretended to be an army for hire, but was really a private militia.

The construction of Orchard City was thus marred by continuous orchestrated attacks that threatened to stop the project ever being completed. There was also a smear campaign, like the 'werewolf venom' lie that had so damaged Orchard Product 1.

Gig's response was threefold.

He halted construction on the northwest version of Orchard City and built it underground in secret in the southeast instead. This necessity as much as an ecological rationale is why all Orchard facilities have that unique 'earthworks' look, extend deep underground and are never more than three storeys high.

He also began a world charm offensive, from hosting the Oscars the year Agent Werewolf won Best Film Adapted From A Computer Game to appearing in a Nollywood extravaganza in which he played himself, badly.

The third aspect of Gig's response to establishment aggression was either genius or the most destructive thing he ever did; possibly both.

The Village

After the fire in the tower I ran back to the countryside. I recognise now that I was looking for perspective through some point of origin, the only time I've ever felt the need.

I ran very fast, leaping great distances to cover ground in the shortest possible time. On the way, I found I could activate a hormone that enabled my fur to reflect light differently, making me almost invisible. This chameleon effect faded, although I didn't realise until I passed through a village.

The village was one of those quaint ones, beloved of a certain type of politician. There was a green, a couple of pubs and a traffic system that could no longer cope, although the roads were empty when I arrived.

The first person I saw was a drunken man, focused on pretending to be sober by walking in a straight line as if he was on a tightrope between two skyscrapers.

"A-right?" he said and I realised I'd been seen.

"Yes thanks," I said. "You?"

"Mustn't grumble," he said, and staggered carefully off.

The encounter gave me confidence, which meant I did not reactivate the invisibility hormone and was smiling when I saw the next man.

His reaction was different. He turned and ran into a wall, bounced off it and then got out a phone, which he dropped.

"You!" he shouted.

"Yes," I said. "Good evening."

A car approached and slowed the way cars do when the driver simply takes her foot off the accelerator and lets entropy do the rest. There were two other women in the car; young, in expensive clothes. One started screaming, the other went to sleep and the driver just kept staring.

The shouty man now had an audience of three attractive women, which complicated things as he tried to think of a way to impress them while dealing with his own terror. He picked up his phone, took a photo of me with it and then dialed a number.

"Baz?" he said. "I'm on the green. Get over here and bring the shotgun."

"There's no need for that," I said.

"Silver!" screamed the woman in the car who was screaming.

The man slapped himself.

"Baz? Bring that candlestick on yer mum's windowsill. No, the silver one."

He ended the call, nodded and smiled as if to reassure me that all would be well.

The screaming woman's voice quickly went hoarse. She jabbed the driver.

"Drive!" she gasped.

The driver accelerated again, but seemed to have forgotten the other activities required to operate a car and headed for the side of a house. I leaped over and pressed my hands against the car's front bumper. The car jolted and stalled.

The screaming woman got out and ran. The driver kept her gaze on me as she eased from the car, opened the rear door and pulled the sleeping woman out. One of the sleeping woman's shoes came off. It was blue and very shiny. The sleeping woman woke up and looked at the shoe as if there was an impossible decision to be made. She left it, kicked the other one off; then she and the driver ran away.

They passed a man running across the green carrying a shotgun and a silver candlestick, which he threw at the first man.

"Baz you tool, throw it at the werewolf!"

"You throw it at the werewolf," Baz screamed. "I'm busy."

He stopped about ten metres away and took aim. I ducked behind the car as Baz opened fire. Glass crashed behind me, followed by more shouts and screams from inside the house. Baz fired again and the car jolted.

"My car!" the driver shouted from some way off.

Baz broke open the shotgun with a loud click. Before he could reload, I jumped over the top of the car and landed in front of him.

"Mate," Baz croaked to the other man, "do something."

The candlestick hit Baz on the side of the head. Baz dropped the shotgun and fell over. The other man ran across, picked up the candlestick and jabbed me with it. Nothing happened, so he jabbed me with it again.

"It's not working," he said, voice thick with indignant grief.

"I'm sorry," I said.

Baz got up, rubbed his head and glared at the first man. We stood there for a bit.

"I'm calling the police!" an elderly lady yelled, waving a whole landline telephone at us from the other side of the shot-out window.

"You should probably take that shotgun home," I told Baz, who nodded.

"I can't get a dial tone," the old woman muttered.

"You've pulled the cable out," I said.

The first man handed Baz the candlestick as the three young women from the car reappeared and stopped nearby.

The one who'd been asleep approached as if her legs were more eager than the rest of her, retrieved the shoes and put them on.

"Limited edition," she said to the Baz and the other man, then shouted "LIMITED EDITION" to me as if I was from abroad and shouting would help with translation.

"Very nice," I said.

"Where are you from?" Baz asked me.

"I don't know," I said.

"Are you an angel?" the driver said.

"He's a werewolf," the formerly screaming woman said, her voice still hoarse. "Hardly angel material, is he?"

"I don't know about being an angel," I said. "I just feel this incredible... love?"

"See?" the driver said. "Angel. He's not a proper werewolf, anyway."

"How do you know what a proper werewolf is, Donna?" the woman who'd been asleep said.

"It's day; there's no full moon," Donna said, "the silver didn't work and he hasn't bitten anyone."

"Oh, I don't do that," I said, before uttering the phrase that would haunt me more than any other: "I'm a lover, not a biter."

From Celebrity Werewolf:
The Biography of Gig Danvers
By Andrew Wallace

Gig's 'Church of Thera' was started by people he met in the village. To begin with, it was more of a fan club; but gradually a creation myth began to emerge. The story had some basis in fact: a male timber wolf bred in a wildlife park escaped at the time of Gig's appearance and was never found. Thera proposed that the wolf was somehow turned into Gig by the Earth itself, which had rather upped its game for its own protection.

Thera did not believe in some giant invisible version of someone's dad in orbit, making up rules about hats. Instead, there was ferocious dedication to equality, science and a responsible approach to free love. Making money was okay; cheating people out of it was not. Ownership was okay; vested interests dating back centuries were not. Hierarchy was okay – so long as everyone put in the same effort and rewards were meaningfully shared – power cliques were not.

In the same way as Gig was not the 'president' of Orchard, so too was he not the 'god' of Thera; neither was he a 'messenger' or any other link to something whose lack of definition justified endless atrocity. Rather, his existence was enough and so, by extension, was the existence of everyone else.

The new religion grew rapidly in opposition to the US evangelicals, whose influence in England had waned now that Orchard Industries had reignited the Kingdom's export economy. Undeterred, the evangelicals bribed their way into the Welsh Protectorate, where they built super-churches that used American tax exemption laws to launder vast sums of money. A fraction of this largesse spread around the Protectorate was enough to create a surveillance-based theocracy that would have been the envy of Old Iran.

Assisted by the ever-helpful Gavin Dergs and his new infrastructure company DIS, the evangelical influence once more became a serious problem for the Kingdom of England. Naturally, Gig Danvers was depicted as the devil incarnate, the Beast on Earth and, worst of all, a fluffy libtard.

Helen Odekumbo and Becky D'Olivera had been following the development of Thera independently of each other. Both suggested to Gig that Orchard do something to assist the fledgling religion as a bulwark against the tide of insanity from the East.

Thera was inadvertently assisted by the Welsh, who ignored the newly imposed authority and destroyed five super-churches in a single night. Although they were made to regret it, their actions bought Orchard valuable time.

Thera received the following: money, organization, Gig himself, Helen Odekumbo's promotional genius and two Orchard Products, one of which the company had been working with for a year prior to launch.

Product 5 was the first organic computer to exceed silicon capacity. Gig had been using it to run Orchard, which to the conventional observer appeared to be chaos. However, free of the old computer model, which was fundamentally just a series of switches, the company could explore organizational structures that extended in multiple dimensions without any loss of control.

The first O5 was the size of a room; the next the size of a large wardrobe. The one in the Thera temple was the size of a cupboard. While the evangelicals struggled with recalcitrant populations using binary methods popular in the Middle Ages, Thera had access to a thought system that opened new possibilities of thought and engagement.

Of course, a computer on its own could only engage so much of the human soul. To go further, something else was needed: the now-infamous Product 6.

She's So High

This world is so beautiful. Every moment I'm here is ablaze with glorious sensation, as if the planet's energies are my own. I know I am lucky to experience it; that people become desensitised to the extraordinary things around them through habit or oppression. It's why I have always wanted to inspire them somehow; to give something back directly.

Orchard is valuable, but its Products take time to develop and are bought and sold as part of an increasingly violent global commerce framework that serves little outside itself. Also, the Products are based on what I am, rather than how I feel.

I tried to get some of this experience across with the concept album, which didn't work very well because everyone except me hates it. I tell myself the concept album is my personal gift to the future, assuming any copies of it survive.

As with everything, I needed help from a friend, so let's look at the act of love and let's look at it with Becky.

There is magic in Becky. Perhaps it's down to her unique understanding of the possibilities in my DNA, or maybe it's our emotional connection, which is so close it's almost a psychic link. I suspect, though, that the source of Becky's magic is that she is Becky.

Whatever the cause, our sex is always astonishing. Both of

us see visions at climax, as if the intensity fuses idea and sensation with such power it feels like our souls have momentarily changed places.

It was after such an experience, in Becky's room in the Midlands Orchard City, that she said, "I think I know a way for us to share this."

We lay on a rucked-up carpet, which was damp with Becky's sweat. I'd like to say we had trashed her place, but it was such a tip already I couldn't tell the difference. In addition, I struggled to determine if the lights I saw were the result of atmospheric illumination, or pleasure so extreme it made my ears ring.

I was thus not best placed to frame a sensible reply.

"Do you mean make our own porn?" I said.

"N– Actually, that's quite a good idea, but no. I mean when we make love, I have some idea of your total experience."

"What's that like for you?" I asked.

"Overwhelming! My senses and emotions are stimulated past anything I've ever felt, or even thought possible."

Her face glowed in the light of an upturned lamp.

"I don't have any loss of control, though," she said. "It's like this... orgasmic, transcendent awareness that resembles a kind of super-empathy."

"Sounds about right," I said.

Becky rested her chin on my chest.

"What if we could synthesise it?" she said. "That way, other people can experience the same incredible things as you."

I felt my jaw go slack and made and effort to shut it again.

"A werewolf drug," I said.

"Yes," Becky said. "Non-addictive, non-toxic – like the soma in Brave New World."

"Wasn't that... bad?"

"The society was bad, Gig. A safe high in ours would be a great help. Besides, I think I know how to do it."

"Oh?"

"It's a by-product of those smart viruses in O5; I hadn't considered it until we made love just now. Look, I never get pregnant, right? It's just not genetically possible. But we're analogous; which is to say we have a profound sexual and emotional entanglement."

"Yes. I love you, Becky."

"I know. Now listen: the O5 works in a similar way; instead of the old switch-based computing system, it uses a sort of viral holistic resonance to create multiple possibilities. Those then engage with existing relationships to arrive at the optimal outcome.

"What's to stop us doing that with the human mind?"

She staggered to her feet and stood there, swaying.

"We know from the antibiotic that your physiology is not only compatible with ours, it's orders of magnitude better. Gig, we are healthier in body because of you; why not be healthier in mind? Oh! Ah!"

"Did you just come again?"

"Yeah! Oh, God, I get it, Gig: I can see it! It's like a cyber-protein! We can control it because it's derived directly from O5 – and needs O5 to operate!"

"An organic computer-controlled drug?"

"Why the hell not? We'll call it hux, after Aldous."

"Excellent choice," I said.

"And we need to make it exclusive."

"I didn't think we were into that, Becky."

"No, sorry; not making myself clear. I mean, we don't want to go to the trouble of creating this thing, only for Gavin Dergs to pinch it as he always does."

"He usually finds a way."

"We need to delay that for longer, this time."

She thought for a moment.

"Gig, did you ever play Second Life or any of the other online games where you're a fantasy warrior, or an elf or something?"

"I'm already a werewolf, so no."

"Right, right. Forgot there for a moment. Maximum soz. Okay. In these games, you accumulate power and wealth – but only in that online realm. We do the same at Orchard with O5, and the payoff is hux."

Becky was smiling now, flushed with excitement as well as pleasure. I nodded, but was unable to stop myself frowning.

"What is it?" Becky said.

"It's just… I always wanted to somehow reach everyone, like with the concept album –"

"We don't talk about the concept album, Gig."

"Well, all right, but it feels limiting to only use hux in Orchard."

"Hmm," Becky said. "What about Thera? You're going to give them O5 to discover the strange new worlds of inner space anyway. With hux, they'll get a lot further."

I stared at her as she grinned down at me.

"Every time I think I've got to the end of your genius…" I said.

"Yeah! Okay, make love to me again will you? But quickly, I've got work to do."

Architecture

Our helicopter lands in the field where I first woke up. The twenty-acre space is roughly trapezoidal: bordered by thick hedgerows, an ancient wood and a steep-banked brook. Seven years ago, there was little to see except grass sown to replenish the soil. Now, Helen waits beside the first temple of the Church of Thera, looking up intently at something I can't see.

Becky and I climb out of the helicopter and walk towards Helen. It's mid-morning in July and sunny, although there was a terrific storm last night. The low-lying temple is undamaged, however, and the sky is fresh and clear, with the last ground moisture burning off into a warm, low haze.

Helen looks exhausted; ill almost. I can tell she has worn her yellow suit for more than a day, which I've not known her do before. Her hair kinks up on one side where she's chewed it: another first. She cannot meet Becky's eye and will not be drawn into one of the conflicts the two of them thrive on.

Instead, Helen mumbles greetings as we follow her into the temple. We are the only ones here; the building was only finished the day before yesterday.

In keeping with the belief system it represents, the temple blends inner and outer space. Part earthwork, part light-touch architecture and part solar energy mechanism, it is light and open. It doesn't point up to some paradoxical entity beyond the clouds, and no structure presents anyone as higher than anyone else. Rather, the temple is grounded: almost a garden, whose maze-like elements guide and reflect.

As we stand and look around, I notice a symbol here and there:

"It's an upside-down A," Becky says.

"No, it's my head," I say. "The sticky-up bits are my ears."

"Yes," Helen says.

Her voice is quiet, as if she is ashamed of it.

"I'm not sure," Becky says. "It's still a shape you could get crucified on."

"In fairness, you could nail someone to just about anything," I say.

"A waterfall?" Helen says. "Fog?"

Despite her tetchiness, she seems on the point of passing out.

"Helen what's wrong?"

"Can we get on with it?" she says.

"It would be better if we were all more... in the mood," Becky says.

"I'm ready when you are," Helen says.

"Have you done the homework?" Becky says.

"Yes, Becky."

Becky smiles and her eyes shine.

"Shall we, then?"

We recline on sculpted mounds covered with grass so thick it feels like upholstery, gazing up through the clear dome at a pale bright sky. Water flows around us as vents guide the air and blend our mixed scent with the smell of grass and wood.

Becky looks as if she's about to make a speech, but instead

shrugs and says, "I'm going in."

She closes her eyes and then opens them, wider this time. "Blimey!"

Becky begins to sing in a language she creates as she sings it. Sometimes the language breaks down into sighs; other times she goes quiet although I can tell the song continues, like a river that dips underground.

Tears trickle down Becky's face as she feels what I feel, directed to that heightened place by Orchards 5 and 6: the first person to go there. From the heat patterns in Becky's body to the sound of her breathing and the way her scent evolves, I can tell the two Products don't impose the new awareness: they reveal it.

And as I realise that, I feel less alone.

Taking a deep and happy breath, I turn to Helen. She sits with her eyes closed, unchanged.

"Helen," I whisper.

Becky turns her enhanced gaze upon Helen, who tightens herself as if we are attacking her.

"Yeah, really good," Helen says, convincing no one.

"It's okay, Helen," Becky says. "It won't hurt you. Join us."

"I have joined you," Helen says.

She is so clenched that her muscles tremble and acid boils in her gut.

"You haven't," I say.

Helen nods as if I haven't spoken.

"It's amazing, man," she says.

Becky reaches for Helen, who doesn't see it coming because her eyes are screwed tight.

"Becky, stop," I say, but it's too late.

Even my speed can't intercept the touch, which affects Helen like a blow to the face.

"Leave me alone!" Helen screams and tries to jump to her feet.

Helen's tight skirt and heels work against her: she stumbles, slipping down the grass bank. As she rolls over, I see her yellow jacket is grass-stained and ripped. Helen stares at the damage to her clothes as if it is a dreadful injury.

"NO!" she screams.

Her hands are claws as she rolls over, the clumsy movement humiliating in this most graceful of women.

Becky jerks back, hands to mouth; then her eyes clear as she disengages from the hux. Helen manages to get to her feet, yanks off her shoes and, still carrying them, sprints from the temple. We go after her.

Helen has the build of a runner, works out every day and moves with the additional speed of the desperate. Becky does her best, but other than sex she does not exercise at all and is quickly out of breath.

"Gig," Becky gasps, "we're going to lose her if you don't give me a lift."

I bend down so Becky can get onto my back, and then I start running.

Temple Grove

Helen has disappeared into the ancient wood. Picking up a deer track three strides in, I stop as I glimpse an expensive yellow shoe sticking out of the undergrowth five metres to my left. Becky shifts as she peers past my head.

The wood has that odd music woods possess: an absence of human sound above a barely perceptible cacophony as flora and fauna go about their unfathomable business. I crouch closer to the ground to inhale the barky scent of earth, lubed metal smell of earthworms and acetone jolt of a chip of the ochre polish Helen painted on her toenails the day before yesterday.

Becky points past the shoe.

"That way?" she whispers.

I shake my head.

"Decoy."

I stand and move off in the opposite direction, following the dense, milky aroma of Helen's naked feet. My pads are tough, but I can still gauge the shape and texture of the ground beneath them: twigs of varying size and antiquity, the remains of leaves, discarded insect carapaces and the suck of muddy soil.

"How big is this place?" I say.

"Five square miles. We should split up."

One of Becky's tweed jacket buttons catches my fur as I let her down; she scrabbles for a second and then I hear her shoes hit the ground. She darts off and we both call for Helen, who does not reply. I cover ground fast, but find nothing amid the pale green gloom of the old wood.

Becky's voice fades and there is silence, broken by her cry from the east. Leaping through the trees, I find her on a knotty outcrop, formed by the roots of a huge tree that leans over the brook.

Last night's storm has left the brook full; its leisurely pace belying depth and power as it surges along a well-worn passage two metres below us. There is movement in the middle of the stream as Helen, who was kneeling under the water, surfaces.

She does not see us; her hair is a shiny streak of black that obscures her face and swings for a moment before it stiffens and begins to curl. The water comes up to her waist, but from the angle of her arms I can tell her hands are folded in her lap. Her eyes are shut tight and knotty tension in her back is visible through the wet blouse.

"Helen?" I call.

Helen puts her hands up behind her streaming hair and covers her face.

Becky takes off her jacket and drops it among the ferns. We climb down to the beach, then wade into the cold, clear water. Becky crouches, slips under the rushing surface and pushes off, gliding close to the pebbly bottom through glinting silvery fish. Helen remains motionless, half-submerged like the statue of a fallen goddess. Becky is just a ripple of movement; then she comes up near the centre, hair framing her face and shining like a helmet as I reach her and Helen.

"Dammit, Helen," Becky says, flicking water from her eyes. "I did all this for you."

Helen pushes her hair back. Washed of its various conditionings, it begins to kink; the little black curls glistening in the tree-filtered sunlight.

"No," Helen says. "You did it for Gig, and for Thera."

"You said you felt apart," Becky says.

"I didn't."

"You did!"

"When?"

"In the slanging match we had after the O1 launch."

Helen stares at Becky.

"That was years ago!" Helen says.

"These things take time," Becky says

"Time," Helen repeats.

"I thought about it and you're right," Becky goes on. "I want Gig to myself and I can't help it, but that's not your fault. We need you. I need you. I don't want you to feel as alone as... you do feel. And this was a way of doing it. So buckle up will you?"

"Oh God, Becky stop it," Helen says, her voice hoarse.

"I can go back to calling you an overdressed admin drone if you like," Becky begins.

Helen seizes Becky and shoves her under the water. I move forward, slowed by the current. Helen's look stops me; then Becky is a gleaming streak as she's hauled up and gripped so tight she cannot move.

"I'm not worthy," Helen whispers through the wet hair covering Becky's left ear.

Becky goes to speak and thinks better of it.

"My surname is Smith," Helen says.

The water flows past us.

"Odekumbo isn't... I made it up, because it sounds African. It isn't even a proper name."

"Helen... Smith?" Becky says.

"Sorry to disappoint your racial expectations," Helen says, letting go of Becky.

"I should think so too," Becky says. She dips her head

back in the water to get the hair out of her eyes and emerges sleek as a seal. "What's the rest of it, then?"

"My birth parents were illegal immigrants," Helen says.

"Hardly your fault."

"My... residential status was never resolved. It turns out my father was not a savoury character. I don't know what happened to him. My mother is still alive, but went back home for some reason. I was fostered, not adopted, so the paperwork was never... It's complicated. An unusual case."

"We have the best lawyers," I say.

"It's too late for that," Helen says. "You see, I didn't know all this myself until Gavin Dergs..."

The wood seems to clench around us, as if in fear.

"How do you know Gavin Dergs?" I say.

"I don't 'know him', Gig!" Helen says. "I was at a meeting last week about the branding for Product 5. It was at an agency rather than one of our buildings. There was a break and afterwards none of the people I'd been talking to came back. Instead, somebody else walked in."

"Dergs?" I say.

"No. One of his Saxon Jihad bully boys. He had documents with him: every piece of evidence, going right back. He told me he'd make it public; that Saxon Jihad would hound me to death and loads of the public would too; you know how it is now. He said... he said there was a way out; if I let him... uh..."

Becky stands up so fast water sprays off her.

"No!" she shouts.

"Dergs knows everything," Helen says. "This guy even knew how I don't like... sex..."

She retches. I put my hand on her shoulder.

"I didn't do it," Helen whispers. "I'm so sorry. I couldn't."

"You've got nothing to be sorry for," I say.

"Yes I do," Helen says. "The Saxon Jihad guy said that if I

wouldn't let him have me then Mr Dergs would take Product 5 instead."

The sounds of the wood are strange around us, as if we have been altered and no longer belong.

"That's the most basic mind game I have ever heard," Becky says. "The whole sex thing was just nonsense."

"No," Helen says. "It worked very well. I mean, I didn't give him Product 5, but that was never their intention. Their intention was to destroy me. And it worked."

"Helen..." I begin.

"I nearly killed myself last night," Helen says. "I had it all set up: a drugs/hot bath/razorblade combo. But..." She giggles. "I couldn't decide what to wear in the bath. Oopsie."

It's as if she's hit my chest with a sledgehammer. I go slack; see Becky's knees bend in senseless shock and reach out to hold her up. I miss her arm; Becky stumbles and for a moment everything is in suspense before she regains her balance in the swirling water.

Helen stares at her rippling reflection with a quizzical look, as if she is part way through the complex solution to a problem she has forgotten. I feel an urgent need to say something, without any idea what it should be. Becky is crying, her face mottled scarlet with anger. I feel the same; rare with me, and I'm not even sure what I'm angry about: Helen for deciding to leave us, or everything that made her want to do it.

"We love you so," I say. "You know we do."

Helen shakes her head.

"You'd think a werewolf would be less palatable than a black woman with the wrong bits of paper," she says.

"That's what we're fighting," Becky says, but her voice has none of its usual fire; she sounds like she's making an excuse.

Helen looks haunted now, her eyes red and expression that of someone just about hanging on, exhausted and increasingly reluctant.

"You just don't know," she says and looks at me. "Not even you."

I reach for Helen, expecting her to pull away but she doesn't. Moving closer, I embrace her; the long, taut limbs an uneasy fit at first. Her shoulders soften a touch, then her head nods forward against me. I hold her tighter, trying to stifle the uncontrollable shudder in my chest; to ignore the wet heat blinding me.

"Don't cry," Helen says.

"I'm not crying," I say, but it comes out 'Blib nut cugug'.

"Silly old wolf," Helen says.

She grips me tight, her strength astonishing. The water in her hair is cold along my muzzle as I hold her, trying to warm her with willpower alone.

"You won't... go, will you?" I finally manage.

I feel her head move as she shakes it.

Pale fingers appear and touch Helen's cheek. Helen turns and gently bites Becky's hand, tugging it for a moment before letting go. There is something inspiring about that movement, and a solution rises through the cold grip of shock. My head lifts from Helen and she looks up at me.

"Is there a deadline for your decision about Product 5?" I ask.

"There's no decision," Helen says. "We can't possibly hand technology like that to a bunch of imbecile Nazis."

"Okay, but you might as well tell us the deadline anyway," Becky says, ringing water from her skirt with partial success.

Helen looks confused.

"Um... Today," she says. "Six o'clock."

"That's eight hours," I say. "Should be time enough."

"For what?" Helen says.

I lift her out of the water.

"For us to solve this with Product 6."

Audio recording of the interview with Paul Belson
Interviewer: Detective Sergeant Sika Patel
Police Station: Paddington Green

BELSON: It's like Invasion of the Body Snatchers. Everyone's gone all gay and that.

DS PATEL: Are you saying Saxon Jihad is now a homosexual organisation?

BELSON: Christ, darling, who stamped your passport? I don't mean literally.

DS PATEL: All I've got to go on is your statement, Paul. You've been arrested for attempting to murder thirty-seven of your former associates by setting fire to the village hall they were meeting in.

BELSON: They betrayed Saxon Jihad!

DS PATEL: Do you confirm you tried to murder them?

[PAUSE]

BELSON: No.

[PAUSE]

DS PATEL: Paul, you were found at the scene with your clothes splashed with petrol. The village hall had petrol poured over it. We have a witness statement from the garage you bought the petrol from and CCTV footage of you buying it. The petrol cans had your fingerprints on, as did the chains and padlock used to secure the village hall so that no one could get out. There was nobody else at the scene other than the people in the hall, each of whom confirms that you have made numerous threats to murder them. We have copies of some of these threats, because they were in writing on social media.

[PAUSE]

BELSON: I've been framed.

DS PATEL: Of course you have.

BELSON: It's true!

DS PATEL: Who's framed you, Paul?

BELSON: The others! The ones in the hall!

DS PATEL: Why would they do that?

BELSON: Because I won't join them.

DS PATEL: In... Saxon Jihad?

BELSON: No, this weird computer drug thing. They're all hooked on it. It's changed them.

DS PATEL: What drug thing?

BELSON: Oh, you'll be hearing about it soon enough, sweetheart. It's that werewolf. He started it.

DS PATEL: What are you talking about?

BELSON: I was at this meeting with Helen Odekumbo, who works with him. We'd found out that she's an illegal. Now, I'm not racist...

DS PATEL: [Sigh]

BELSON: ...but it's got to be a fair system, right?

DS PATEL: Where did you get the information about Helen Odekumbo?

BELSON: I'm afraid I cannot reveal that.

DS PATEL: You've been arrested for attempted mass murder. Think again.

BELSON: It's got nothing to do with... what you arrested me for.

DS PATEL: Paul–

BELSON: I've got family, right? I can't tell you. Please.

DS PATEL: All right, Paul. You had information about Helen

Odekumbo. What form did this information take?

BELSON: Original paper documents. I told Helen that Saxon Jihad would make them known if she didn't... er... That is, if she didn't let us have details of the werewolf's new invention.

DS PATEL: What invention?

BELSON: O5. It's their latest computer.

DS PATEL: So you attempted to blackmail Helen Odekumbo.

BELSON: No. I did blackmail her.

DS PATEL: You admit that?

BELSON: Yes.

DS PATEL: I see. Go on.

BELSON: We gave her some time to think about it, expecting she'd say no and we'd be able to discredit her, but she told us to meet her at that temple of Thera they've got near Wadhurst in Kent.

DS PATEL: Why there?

BELSON: The new computer isn't like a laptop; it's more a virtual thing powered by this machine the size of a cupboard. There's only a few of them so far, and one is at the temple. Naturally we thought it was a trap, so ten of us went; but when we arrived there were only three people there.

DS PATEL: Who were they?

BELSON: Helen Odekumbo and this other woman, Becky Dolly something; proper mentalist but well horny if you know what I mean.

DS PATEL: Rebecca D'Olivera?

BELSON: That's her.

DS PATEL: Who else from Orchard Industries was at the temple?

BELSON: Him. The werewolf.

DS PATEL: Gig Danvers.

BELSON: Yes.

DS PATEL: What happened?

BELSON: They made us welcome, told us they were happy to give us the computer but that it wasn't a physical thing; more an experience we would be able to share with whoever we wanted. Then Helen told us to lie back on these grassy mound things inside the temple and I went, 'So that massive talking dog can bite us? Jog on.'

DS PATEL: You didn't take part, then?

BELSON: No, only half the lads did, the rest of us stood guard.

DS PATEL: And was anyone bitten?

BELSON: No.

DS PATEL: So how did the computer work? Were there... electrodes or something?

BELSON: No. You drink it.

DS PATEL: Drink...? Okay. What happened then?

BELSON: Nothing for a while, then George starts doing this odd sort of singing and the next thing they're all at it. Very peculiar. Then Carlos begins to cry and goes over to Helen and says he's sorry about everything; how he can see eternity and she's in it and he wants to join her.

DS PATEL: What did Helen say to that?

BELSON: She didn't seem to know what to say, just kept looking at the other two. Eventually, Carlos wanders off around the temple talking in code, like maths or something – as if he understands bloody maths, which frankly, Detective Sergeant Patel, he does not.

[PAUSE]

At least, he didn't use to.

DS PATEL: Did anyone film this process?

BELSON: I did, but it wouldn't work. It's while I was faffing around with my phone camera that Carlos got out. That temple has loads of ways in and he snuck off to the van, got all the documents we had on Helen and burned them.

DS PATEL: So the drug that they drank –

BELSON: They didn't drink the drug, they drank something like a… an interface with the new computer. The drug is separate. It lives in the system. Normally you have to earn access to it, but they'd jigged it in some way.

DS PATEL: So, you're saying that the Orchard team used the drug to brainwash Carlos into destroying the documents?

[PAUSE]

BELSON: I want to say yes, but I don't think so. See, afterwards, Becky told me that the drug just gives you the same sensations the werewolf has all the time; how he's so full of love and understanding that it breaks down hatred and ignorance.

DS PATEL: But you didn't want that.

BELSON: The others did. They're like different people now. But someone has to stay true to the cause, right?

DS PATEL: Why?

BELSON: Because that's what a cause is.

DS PATEL: And because Gavin Dergs backs Saxon Jihad and you're scared of him.

BELSON: I'm not… I…

[PAUSE]

You don't know him. What he's like. What he can do.

DS PATEL: You've met him, then?

BELSON: I... not exactly.

DS PATEL: Have you heard from Gavin Dergs since events at the Thera temple?

BELSON: No.

DS PATEL: I take it no one passed technical details of the O5 computer to Gavin Dergs or any of his other associates?

[PAUSE]

BELSON: No.

DS PATEL: And Saxon Jihad is, to all intents and purposes, no longer in existence.

BELSON: It's like we formed to fight the beast, but the beast just wasn't up for it and... and...

[PAUSE]

I really didn't go to kill the others. I bought the petrol and the chains, but those were for this quad biking team my kid's part of and... I don't often see him and... It's him I thought I was going to meet, but he wasn't there. It must have been while I was looking for him that they doused the petrol around and put the chain on, then called you lot. I only got petrol on me from trying to get in the village hall.

DS PATEL: But they were all locked in the hall.

BELSON: They could have left a window open or something.

DS PATEL: A window. Right.

BELSON: It's true! One of 'em must have got back in through it once they'd poured the petrol everywhere, then closed the window after himself.

DS PATEL: Bit risky though, isn't it? What if someone lit a cigarette?

BELSON: None of them smokes. I mean, some used to but not now; not since the temple.

DS PATEL: A light switch turned on, then. That can ignite a building full of fumes.

BELSON: No. The village hall was dark. And I bet they called you on a landline, so no sparks from a mobile either. Plus, the fire brigade turned up as well. Did you call them?

DS PATEL: I… er…

BELSON: It was the others. They took a risk, yes, but they controlled it.

[PAUSE]

You know what scares me?

DS PATEL: What scares you, Paul?

BELSON: The lads didn't use to be clever. They'd never have had the nous to frame me before, but now… Now…

[PAUSE]

Oh, God. I've had it, haven't I?

The Launch of Orchard Product 8
By Otis Pyke-Jones
Mummy At Large

I was at the launch of the first Orchard Product ten years ago. It shames me how I bought into the 'werewolf venom' rumour, although Gig was as generous about it as he is about everything. I'd already decided not to publish the story, when he called and told me that as it was going to break anyway I should go ahead.

It would probably have made my career, but I didn't do it. I've always been loyal to Gig, although not uncritically. He can take it, though; he's not a dictator like those on the other side.

Because it is sides, now. People tend to be with the World Party, which aligns itself with Orchard; or the Englander Party, which is backed by the US evangelicals, Gavin Dergs and the local fascists. The Englanders must have short memories, after what happened to Wales.

Against such a background, something spectacular was needed, and last night we got it.

I've been to every Orchard launch and this one was by far the most outrageous; the most theatrical. You can even break it down into three acts, as follows:

ACT ONE

Gig Danvers is an incredible warm-up act, even though the feature he is usually warming the crowd up for is himself. We thought he was just going to open the new Orchard Academy, which covers fifty square kilometres of Cornwall; then we thought it was the ten-thousand seat arena, which was packed, and which would have been amazing enough.

Instead, he left a long pause and said, 'Tonight, we launch Product 8'.

I tell you, the response to that one line made every stadium rock concert I've ever been to look like a tea party at the vicarage.

'You're going to love it,' he said from the front of his vast new arena, when the clamour finally died down.

Then he lifted off the stage and flew over us.

That's right: a flying werewolf, as if we haven't got enough to be dealing with. Even my head boggled at it, and I named my son Gig.

Despite no obvious means of staying airborne, Gig's flight was very smooth. Sometimes he moved as if he was standing, his feet three metres above us. Other times he flew like Superman and even did the pose with his right fist. I think it was meant to be funny, although everyone was too astonished to laugh.

Eventually, he landed, said, 'Okay, thanks for coming,' and walked off the stage.

ACT TWO

There was silence, then the house lights came up and everyone looked at each other. After an awkward pause people began to get up, grumbling about werewolves. Then the lights went down again and Gig strode back onstage, grinning like an impresario.

'You're probably wondering,' he said, 'what on Earth that was all about.'

'Yes!' someone shouted and I realised it was me.

Gig smiled.

'Earth is the word,' said Gig and he wasn't smiling anymore. 'Let me show you how I did it.'

He held out one of those beautiful, terrifying clawed hands.

'String,' he said.

But his hand was empty.

'Can you see it?' said Gig. 'No? How about now?'

The entire wall behind him lit up. It was a screen, which showed a live image of Gig's hand. The dark flesh was hard, like black bone, and there were no pores or other patterns. It was as if there was a smooth, undulating landscape behind Gig: another planet, far from the sun.

We zoomed in closer.

'Magnification times 1,000,' said Gig.

Still nothing.

'5,000.'

Blackness.

'10,000.'

There! A filament so fine it appeared to be made of light, like a tiny crack in reality.

'All Orchard Products are derived from my physiology,' said Gig, 'and this string is based on the structure of my fur. A single strand was enough to lift me off the stage; three more to enable the flight you witnessed earlier.

'In addition, the superstring conducts both data and electricity. It does not tangle or snare, and retains its strength and conductivity regardless of how long it is.'

He regarded us with an expression I haven't seen before.

'Please remain seated.'

Covers on the windows fell away. Even the roof slid open

to reveal a calm summer evening, with a sunset of scarlet and gold. Structures I had thought were support mechanisms over the arena's rounded corners suddenly flexed, and I realised they were cranes.

People gasped as the view outside changed; the perspective altering as we saw more and more of Orchard Academy: its buildings and parks; its gardens and transport systems. And there, beyond the new forests, the blue-black hammered beauty of the sea.

The cranes telescoped smoothly to lift us and we rose fast: ten storeys in less than a minute. More tiny cables must have steadied the great mass, because the arena didn't swing at all. I noticed the floor was transparent with a clear view right to the ground.

Gig walked across the stage and climbed to a pulpit halfway up the left wall. When the stage rose, folded into the ceiling and disappeared, I realised he didn't want anything to obstruct what he was going to show us.

ACT THREE

'There are many applications for this product,' said Gig, 'but there was one that was the most urgent and the most inspiring.'

There were no projections of Gig now; just his amplified voice. To most of the others, he was a tiny figure, a little grey stick werewolf.

'I...'

Gig's voice cracked. He looked down, took a deep breath and pointed out to sea.

'There,' he said.

A mile offshore, the ocean began to glow. At first it was a smudge of red light that went orange as steam billowed around it. Soon the light was an almost blinding white, although I'm sure no one looked away.

Out of the brightness rose a sleek, silver shape.

'We call these events launches,' said Gig. 'This time it's actually true.'

The silver rocket eased from the surface of the sea towards the sky, picking up speed as it rode its dazzling torch into the night.

'What makes this launch different,' said Gig, 'is that our rocket is still attached to the Earth.'

He leaned forward in his pulpit.

'Out there is a platform, like a low-slung oil rig, with a reel of superstring at each corner. Cables from each reel form an X and in the centre of the X is the rocket, carrying those cables a hundred thousand kilometres up into space. Once there, the rocket will open solar sails to become the anchor for a space elevator.

'We call that space elevator the Beanstalk, my friends.'

There was some applause; less this time, because everyone was staring at the rocket and wondering if it was going to reach its destination.

'The Beanstalk is a cheap, safe and regular means of getting into space,' said Gig. 'Unconstrained by the weight restrictions, hazards and the enormous financial and environmental cost of conventional rocketry, we can assemble space vehicles and other facilities at the top of the elevator, and maintain supplies to them as well.'

The height seemed to clutch at me and I swayed in my seat. I imagined trying to catch hold of an impossibly slender cable as the enormous drop yawned beneath. Gig's voice brought me back.

'Our understanding of this world and others will expand like never before,' he said, 'and not only that. Solar energy and access to the rest of the planets in the Solar System, as well as raw materials from the asteroid belt, can be ours with minimal risk and expense.

'Our own Earth need no longer take the strain. She has done enough.'

There was huge applause this time; especially from people wearing Thera designs. Gig smiled. He still looked weary, though.

'Originally, we thought the platform should be sited along the equator for stability,' he said. 'However, with a cable this strong, we can take the strain despite our position. We had similar fears about tidal influences from the sun and moon, but we have found that my unique physiology automatically nullifies those effects. Then there's the chance of orbital collisions, and I can assure you that the rocket will be able to deflect any of these. It incorporates a state of the art Orchard 5 computer to assist with manoeuvres and detection.

'Finally, a cable might catch and swing the rocket back to the Earth.'

The window behind Gig became a screen and we saw the view down the rocket as it left the planet's atmosphere.

'We'll be all right, though,' said Gig.

Only people who know him well would have picked up the strain in Gig's voice, and I noticed for the first time how he looked less wiry now than gaunt. It's possible that of all the stresses and attacks he has dealt with, the pressure of launching Product 8 has been the most destructive.

What a gamble to have taken! If Gig's enemies shot that rocket down… But the risk would be greater for them, wouldn't it? Oh God, here was history being made and it was hard work just existing in the terrible uncertainty of it.

And yet the cables held, and the rocket deployed as Gig said it would. Champagne appeared from somewhere and I gulped it down, barely able to stand. People brought more. They were all happy.

I couldn't see Gig anywhere, and decided to find him. My

bandage outfit has evolved over the years and accommodates spectacles, a midriff-tightener and built-in trainers. The latter were particularly useful as booze fought shock for control of my tottering equilibrium.

People spoke to me and I think I said the right things as I looked for Gig, convinced he wasn't far because the arena was still airborne. Suddenly inspired, I checked behind some raised seating and sure enough, there he was. I didn't talk to him though, because he was on his knees, weeping in Becky's arms.

Nightmare

I don't just attend Orchard parties. There are also events such as the annual fancy dress shindig held at the Dorchester by one of the charities that has replaced the government welfare department.

Fancy dress is awkward for me. In theory I don't need to do much, but I can't be seen not to make an effort.

It always backfires. The first year I went as Lassie, which no one got because the orange dye didn't take and I had to go back out and get a wig. Then there was the time I went as Anubis and an Egyptian man took offence, although it turned out his girlfriend had dumped him because she fancied me.

Tonight, I think I've cracked it. I stand apart from everyone else and enjoy the laughter, of which there seems to be more than usual.

Becky struts up. Undeterred by the Anubis experience, she has come as Cleopatra: hair a black bob and eyes magicked into glittering hieroglyphs.

"Gig, what are you meant to be?"

I draw myself up.

"The Dark Knight," I say.

"You look like a giant fruit bat in a dress," Becky says.

"I do not!" I say. "Do I?"

I look in an ornamental mirror.

"Ah," I say.

"Couldn't Helen have sorted this out?"

'Helen is trying to be less controlling," I explain. "She says it makes us predictable."

A waiter stops beside us with a tray of filled champagne glasses. Becky downs them one after another and then strides off. I look at the waiter; evidently as confused as I am, he just shrugs.

I head onto the balcony for London's version of fresh air. Closing the doors behind me, I cross to the railing that overlooks the road, where I spread my black cape and growl, "I'm Batman" to the rushing night.

I let go of the cape and wind blows it in my face. I struggle and knock over a plant, then haul the cape and mask off and throw them to one side.

There is the sound of slow clapping, to my left. I turn as Gavin Dergs walks across the balcony towards me, a yellow grin on his ratty face.

"Now that was funny," Gavin says.

I have finally met him, and find he disgusts me. It's as if he smells terrible, like a living corpse that has rolled in excrement. He is compact but not tall, although for some reason I feel that we're eye to eye. His dark grey pinstripe is exquisitely tailored, yet still contrives not to suit him, as if he's stolen it. The skin is sallow, thin and older than it should be, as if he has some wasting disease. His black eyes do not reflect light.

Despite the loathsome clarity of Gavin's appearance, I find him difficult to focus on, as if he exists at a higher frequency. His gleeful malevolence is almost a physical trait. Neither mentally ill or psychologically atypical, he is unknowable: almost viciously alien.

I recall a quotation about evil being banal, but this is evil as power: power that lives between the cracks of what we will and won't admit, what we will and won't tolerate, what we can and can't understand.

"How did you get in?" I say.

Gavin smiles.

"I'm a white man in a suit," he says. "I can go where I like."

"You should use that power for good," I say.

"How?" he says.

The question surprises me. For a moment, I can't think of anything.

"We could work together," I say.

"We do work together, Gig! You invent something; I rip it off."

"Why?" I ask him.

"My wealth is ten times yours," Gavin says, his smugness like choking fog.

"You're doing this for more money than you can spend?" I say.

He glares at me.

"Oh, I can spend it, Gig."

I look him up and down.

"On what, exactly?" I say.

"Time is shorter than everyone realises," Gavin says. "I need to have everything in place, before…"

He stops himself.

"Before what?"

"Wars over water," Gavin says.

He means something else; I wait for him to continue, but he just stares at me. I look back into the party, which seems set in another world, and sense Gavin follow my gaze.

"You waste your time trying to save everyone, no matter how useless they are," Gavin says. "I have no such debilitating sentimentality"

"You're a parasite," I say, the unkindest thing I have ever said to anyone.

"No, Gig. I am a predator."

"So says every vicious male inadequate since the word 'predator' was invented."

"I'm hardly inadequate," Gavin says, with that stillness people employ when they don't want you to know you've enraged them.

"Predators aren't meant to destroy everything."

"Predators don't care either way, not that you'd know."

"Everything you do is wrong," I say. "Everything you do is evil."

"If I'm so evil then kill me now," Gavin says.

I go to speak before I properly understand him; then stop myself and blink repeatedly instead.

"Go on," Gavin continues. "Your natural weapons are the envy of the military world. What are you waiting for?"

"It's not... I —"

"You think you can be as powerful as you are and remain good?" Gavin says.

I feel as if the hotel has lurched, and my senses will not catch up.

Just one line comes:

"I'm a lover," I say, "not a biter."

Gavin looks pained.

"You don't have to bite me," he says, and then brightens as if helpful suggestions are occurring to him. "You could rip me in half, swing me around and dash my brains over the balcony, or punch my head off."

"No," I say.

Gavin's expression mingles amusement and contempt.

"Who is more evil?" he says. "The one who does bad things or the one who refuses to stop him?"

"No," I say again; it's all I can manage.

"I think you are putting your principles before the good of the Kingdom, Mr Danvers! Shame on you."

I grip the metal railing; it warps in my hand like warm toffee as Gavin laughs. I crouch to defend myself, but against what? Laughter? Since when did it hurt this badly?

Still laughing, Gavin turns and walks away.

Mummy At Large

I go to see Otis in hospital. He is in his own room, swathed in plaster and bandages; even his face is almost obscured.

"Well," I say to him, "this is ironic."

"I thought that," Otis says, his voice muffled.

I go to pat some part of him that isn't covered but there isn't anywhere, so I touch his shoulder lightly and then sit in the chair by the bed.

"What happened?" I say.

"I followed up a lead on the Dergs organisation."

"Not wise, Otis. We talked about this."

"I can't ignore it," Otis says. "He's genuinely evil."

Otis gasps, presses a button to release what smells like morphine, then lies quietly for a while.

"I must have got too close," he says, his voice dreamier, "because some of his goons found me and…"

"I'm so sorry that happened."

"It was worth it."

"Why?" I say.

"I found something, Gig."

I want to know, and yet also don't. Otis shifts; even through the drug haze, his worry and frustration are evident.

"Is the Beanstalk operational yet?" he asks.

"No," I say. "The cables aren't thick enough to provide

traction. We're growing additional layers up them, like sheaths."

Otis sighs.

"It might be too late," he says.

"Why?"

"Because Dergs has got something better."

I experience an unseemly moment of indignation.

"Better?" I say.

"Sorry."

"We're supposed to be the clever ones," I say. "Normally, he just copies us."

"Not this time."

"What is it you think he's got?"

"A hyperspace chamber."

I blink at Otis, unsure if I've heard correctly through the bandages.

"It's made up," I say.

"That was my view, but now I'm not so sure."

I scratch my head.

"Does hyperspace even exist?" I say.

"There's a theoretical layer beneath normal space that can be used to short-cut vast stellar distances," Otis says, "although you wouldn't use a 'chamber' on Earth for that.

"But there's another definition: a different kind of space, perhaps informed by a different kind of time. This device could be how Gavin Dergs constantly has the jump on you. If we could find it…"

"… and destroy it –"

"Steal it, Gig! How much have they stolen from us? From you, I mean."

"I'm just not sure about that… solution," I say.

"At least let's find out what this thing is," Otis says.

I think about it.

"All right."

"We need to be careful, though, as you can see from my present situation."

"I doubt I'll have that trouble," I say.

Otis forgets his condition and goes to sit up; he cries out and I put a hand on his bandaged chest.

"You're not going, Gig," he says before I can speak. "You're too valuable."

"Otis –"

"What if the chamber can be used as a weapon? It might be something even you can't withstand."

"Okay," I say, saddened at the ease with which I now lie.

Otis calms down. I lean back in the chair and wait for his breathing to even out.

"Did you get a location?" I say.

"That's the weird thing," Otis says. "It's in one of the Orchard properties."

Astonished, I stare at him.

"The City Academies?" I say.

"No, one of the smaller buildings in London. You run a couple of sub-companies through it."

"Which building?"

"The Light Exchange in Ropemaker Street."

Skywolf

Simply walking in to the Light Exchange would attract attention; even with the invisibility hormone I'd be noticed. Besides, I love the Skywolf.

I rarely have time for hobbies, but one I've developed involves four Orchard Products adapted for my sole use. The Skywolf resembles one of the smaller rifles like the SA80, and is made from a transparent version of my claw material. There's an Orchard battery in the stock next to the latest O5 pocket computer and a motorised five-kilometre roll of superstring.

The barrel has sensors to determine distance, height and obstructions; it ends with a small suction cup that has a smart-grip as great as mine. Scanners check for air traffic, wind direction and strength, while a laser enhances the tubular magnification sighting.

I look through it across London at the Light Exchange; home of Gavin Dergs's mysterious hyperspace chamber. Although the Light Exchange is a kilometre away, the sighting reveals how the building's impressive pale marble cladding is chipped in places.

It's two in the morning, but lights are on in about a third of the offices. Forty storeys tall, the Light Exchange is half as high again as the roof of this empty housing block.

A ping in my earpiece lets me know the rifle has completed its calculations, so I pull the trigger. There's not much recoil as the suction cup vanishes on its bullet-fast journey to the window-cleaning frame around the top of the Light Exchange. Another ping indicates the sucker is fixed. I unfold a second handgrip from the stock, get a good hold of it and step onto the roof ledge. The street below is deserted, but I activate the invisibility hormone anyway.

I jump and pull the trigger.

A vertiginous thrill shudders through me as the motor spools the cable in at speeds calculated to utilise the inertia of my fall. Wind rushes my fur, while the city's layered drone is studded with car horns and alarms. Lead and electricity, a cabbage baseline of garbage and the human animal scent of millions are almost visible motes in the hot night. I'm pulled between glass canyons over the cityscape towards the Light Exchange, which enlarges like it's leaping at me.

I imagine a werewolf-shaped hole in the glass; however, the Skywolf has accommodated this likelihood and slows. I begin to swing; then the motor re-engages at higher speed and I shoot up the front of the building. Lit windows alternate with dark, like a binary data pattern slipping by too fast to understand.

The motor slows again, then stops, and I hang forty storeys above the street. Climbing onto the frame, I disengage the suction pad, sling the Skywolf onto my back and jump down to the deserted roof.

I've had the building's alarm turned off, and the access system altered to accommodate a master-key instruction in the Skywolf O5. I use it now and the roof door springs open.

Building schematics have revealed there are only three places the hyperspace chamber can be. None of them are in Gavin's name or that of any Dergs company. The most likely location is an electrical switch room that controls power for the top half of the building, despite inexplicable 'back-up' facilities on two other levels.

Moving silently through deserted workplaces, I find dim stairwells and offices in darkness. A few lights are always on, though, and reveal shadowy glimpses of people's lives: a cactus on a terminal, a cardigan on a chair; a sign about washing up. Passing stores and meeting rooms, I spot a couple embracing in a corridor. To avoid them, I ease into an extract duct that takes me straight to the switch room.

The hyperspace chamber is not here; it's empty apart from three large electrical cabinets in the centre. The cabinets are padlocked, so I use a claw to get one open. A diagram on the door shows the entire distribution board supporting a single ring main, which routes power six floors down. I get the other cabinets open and find the same configuration, with enough electrical output to power the building.

I close and lock the cabinet doors, then pull myself back up into the extract duct. I slip along it, but when I get six floors down I find the way blocked. Other, smaller ducts run off in all directions to ensure the duct functions as it should, but the hyperspace chamber clearly has its own discrete air supply to go with its dedicated power.

I back up, open another access hatch and drop into a corridor. This one is familiar; I've been here on my own and with Becky. I hesitate, gripped by a visceral terror that feels like the whole building is watching me, waiting; its black eyes widening in sick delight.

For a long moment, I can't move and almost fall. Putting my hand against a door to steady myself, I know at once that the hyperspace chamber is on the other side. I fumble, drop the Skywolf with a clatter and freeze.

No doors burst open; no guards appear and no weapons fire. Wondering why I would fear any of those things, I pick up the rifle and hold it to the door. I half hope it won't work, but the door swings open.

Motion-activated lights reveal a short corridor leading to what looks like a hotel room. There's a bed, desk and wardrobe. The curtains are drawn. I walk in, unsure, then peer under the bed and find an access hatch.

I push the bed and it slides away. The Skywolf will not open the hatch, so I yank it off its hinges.

The awful smell from below is like a billowing darkness. Even breathing through my mouth doesn't dampen the horror; I can taste it under the acidic industrial stink of strenuous attempts at cleaning.

Blood: old and new, from many different people.

I want to run, but instead creep down metal stairs into the septic gloom. There's no motion-activated light, but that's not surprising: Gavin Dergs would want to control the imposition of darkness. At the bottom of the stairs, I find a wall switch and click it on.

I expected some uncanny engine; a stargate perhaps, or frenzy of lashed-together steampunk genius. Instead, the place looks like a CCTV control room: circular, with half the wall space filled with large monitors, all switched off. There are six metal keyboards with reinforced keys spread across a long steel desk that follows the perimeter of the room.

Indeed, the whole place is metal, from the chequer-plate floor to the high ceiling. It's battered, too, as if something has repeatedly exploded in here; denting and scraping the steel walls.

The lights have been replaced recently; there are old fitting holes, badly filled with resin. There is no subtle shading, though; everything is dazzlingly bright. The industrial smell comes from nozzles in the ceiling: an automated washing system, to rinse away... What?

I turn and see the trolleys. They look as if they're from a morgue: heavy, stainless steel and long enough for a person. I push one; it moves easily on well-oiled wheels, even though the trolley is dented and old. All three trolleys have got thick plastic straps, which are open.

I get my nausea under control and analyse the smell. It's not just blood; other substances hide under the cleaning chemicals. There are different mixes of female and male pheromones, sweat and occasionally desire. It's mainly fear, though, and given the excremental base notes, utter terror. Some are faint and scored with decay, so whatever happens in here has been happening for a long time.

There is another scent, under the blood and horror: a weird, burning aroma like spent fuel. I look at the battered walls and try to imagine what unearthly force erupted in here.

Backing away from the trolleys, I turn and tap a key on one of the six boards.

The screens light up with a basic corporate operating package and an email account with empty in and out boxes. Clicking on the browser directs me to Gavin's latest search engine: the same as his last two, but with a different logo. The search history is blank; the trash folder is empty and I can't find any documents. I try the other terminals, but they are the same. There are no additional panels in the walls, and cabinets under the screens contain nothing but standard, silicon-based computers.

I think of me and Becky asleep nearby and shudder as if I might fall apart.

Smacking off the light switch, I sprint up the stairs. My arms become visible, so I reactivate the invisibility hormone. Soon, I'm going too fast to stop in time for the doors in my way and crash through them, trying not to scream as I go.

From Celebrity Werewolf:
The Biography of Gig Danvers
By Andrew Wallace

The Beanstalk launch sent an already weakened global economy into freefall. Gold had long been abandoned as the means of fixing values that fluctuated by the nanosecond, so alternatives were developed and discarded in a form of high-speed financial evolution.

The Kingdom of England responded with characteristic inventiveness, and pegged its economy to Gig Danvers himself. Even if Gig was not, as some people suspected, immortal, then he was certainly as robust as metals whose value had been determined by how shiny they were. He was given the official title of 'Royal Protector', despite Helen Odekumbo's quickly justified warning that the name made Gig sound like an extremely large guard dog.

Thera came into its own, having blended with Orchard Industries to provide a moral as well as commercial backup to Gig's position as de-facto national figurehead. Meanwhile, sterling made its exit from the world stage, to be replaced with the L (for Lupus) and the upside-down **A** symbol that represented Gig himself. Given how many economies now relied on Orchard Products, the Kingdom's decision had the desired effect of calming the markets for long enough to achieve stability.

As with any deal of this kind, however, there was a terrible cost.

Halloween

"They want you to marry that princess," Helen says.

"Which one?" I ask.

"That one probably," Becky says.

She points at a dark-haired young woman with honey-coloured skin dressed as... I'm not sure if it's a witch or a dominatrix. Either way, there are many zips.

We're at the Orchard Academy Halloween Party. The huge, circular park in the centre has been lit in orange and green, with stilt walkers and acrobats moving through the cheerful, eerie space. In the distance, the Beanstalk's thickening trunks gleam as they stretch up into darkness.

"Really?" I say. "Um..."

"We all know you love Becky," Helen says, "but this marriage would be hugely symbolic."

"Isn't it enough that I'm Royal Protector?" I say.

"No," says Helen.

"Would you mind if I married her?" I ask Becky.

"Of course I would," Becky says.

"For God's sake!" Helen shouts.

Becky's jaw clenches.

"It's just a... soap opera thing," I tell her.

"People base political decisions on soap operas," Helen says. "They're very important."

Otis pops up from behind a bush.

"Can I put that in my blog?" he says.

"How long have you been there?" Helen says.

"Fifty-six minutes," I say.

"Fifty-eight," says a someone who sounds like a younger version of Otis.

"Who's that?" Becky says.

"Gig Junior," Otis says.

A young man aged about sixteen stands up next to Otis. Both are wearing bandages, and I get the feeling that Gig Junior is wearing one of his father's hand-me-downs. Thankfully, Otis long ago ran out of his cremated grandmother.

"Get out of that bush, you idiots," Becky says.

They come over. Becky produces a magnum of champagne; I swipe the top off with a claw and Helen finds glasses. Otis pours and we all drink.

"To Prince Gig!" says Gig Junior.

"You make me sound like a concert," I say.

Everyone laughs, except Becky, whose eyes are shining.

"I'm not going to marry that princess, Becky," I say.

"You probably should," Becky says.

She too is wearing a witch outfit; a more traditional one: long dress, too much black eye makeup and hair everywhere. I go to speak, but can't because I'm too happy.

"Cheers," I manage.

Becky nods and stares at her drink.

Turning to Helen, I notice a growing tension in my chest. As I watch bubbles rise through the champagne, I realise Becky thinks I was toasting the idea of marrying someone else. When I go to speak to her again, she has gone.

I mumble excuses and head off to look for her. Years of experience have made Becky adept at avoiding me when she wants to, so I may be searching for a while.

A high, hedgerow maze looks like the kind of place she would go for one her ferociously erotic sulks. It's away from the main party, so I lope at a comfortable speed, getting to the heart of it in moments.

Becky isn't there, though. Gavin is.

He sits on a driftwood bench, wearing a Dracula costume. It suits him.

"Gig!" he cries, loathsome joy stretching his face. "Fancy seeing you here!"

My claws extend of their own volition; I retract them, with effort. Gavin does not look impressed.

"Do sit down, O Royal Protector," he says.

I remain standing.

"You're not richer than me any more," I say.

"Hm? Oh. No. But that's okay."

"What do you want?"

"Same thing I always want, Gig: to spoil your party."

"You already have."

Gavin laughs.

"Such grumpiness!" he says. "Becky run off, has she?"

"Shut up about Becky," I say.

There is wonder in Gavin's eyes.

"How you must love her," he says. "Have you ever had sex with anyone else?"

"No."

"Becky has."

"I don't own her."

"Getting on rather, isn't she? Never was much cop to look at but so sexy, hmm?"

It's a relief to walk away from him.

"Lovely to see you, Gavin."

"Don't you want to know how I got in here?" he says, voice rising behind me with unexpected desperation.

"I don't care, Gavin. Enjoy the champagne. Try to make

some friends."

"I'm the only one you don't love," Gavin says.

For some reason, this truth makes me hesitate.

"And you're the only one I don't hate," Gavin adds.

I turn back to him.

"You hate everyone?"

He nods, his black eyes bright.

"I'm sorry to hear that."

"Don't be!" Gavin says. "It's how I am; how I'm made."

He seems to expect an understanding. I shrug slowly and spread my hands.

"Look at the moon, Gig."

The moon is a bright curve.

"Very nice," I say.

"No," Gavin says. "It's not."

"Why, what have you done to it?"

"Nothing. It's what it's done to me, and to you."

"It hasn't done anything to me, Gavin."

"Oh, Gig…"

As he goes to speak, his expression distorts. He's crying and is astonished by it; enraged, as if it's an infection. His lower lip trembles and the vicious irony goes out of his face.

"For so long…" he manages, "I wanted to… And now…"

He jumps up and again I get the feeling he's the same height as me.

"You saw the hyperspace chamber," he says.

"Yes."

"It's not the only one."

His eyes are stretched wide, as if he is trying to transmit a truth too awful even for him.

"They're in every one of your properties, Gig," Gavin says. "Your precious Orchard Cities, your buildings and towers; everywhere you go there is a hyperspace chamber."

"It's just a kind of office," I say. "It's not a hyperspace

chamber at all."

"It is!" Gavin shouts. "Time passes differently there."

"You kill people there," I say. "I couldn't get enough evidence to prove –"

"Yes, yes," Gavin says. "But you had to see it. You have to know."

"Why do you kill them?"

Gavin blinks at me as if the answer is obvious.

"Food," he says.

The terrible fear sickness is back. I look up at the moon to hide my tears.

"Don't be sad, Gig," Gavin says. "It's really not your fault."

"How could it be my fault you're a cannibal?" I say.

He gives me another odd look, as if he expects me to understand his evil.

"Have you ever seen a living fly in a spider's web?" Gavin says.

"Yes," I say.

"The way the intensity of the fly's buzz increases as the spider approaches, using every joule of energy to try and get away?"

"Oh Gavin, please, stop…"

"Now imagine the human version –"

"Stop it!"

He stares at me.

"I need them in that condition to sustain me," he says.

I close my eyes, steady my breathing; open them again.

"Who were they?" I say.

"Precious ones," Gavin says. "To me, at any rate; to society: nobody. That's why they're not missed. Some are criminals, Gig, horrible criminals –"

"Like you?"

"I'm not a criminal, Gig."

"You're a murderer."

"You wouldn't say that about a tiger."

"You're hardly that."

"On one level I am," Gavin says. "I don't have a choice about my... diet."

"There will be an alternative —"

"There isn't!"

He gets himself under control.

"A thief, then," I say.

Gavin sniggers.

"Hardly," he says.

He looks as if he wants me to get a joke he has not yet told.

"Who else have you... consumed?" I say.

Gavin thinks about it.

"Junkies," he says. "Although not many because they tend to be physically degraded."

"Are they less tasty?"

His face twists and I feel a flush of triumph.

"Don't be facetious, Gig," he says. "It doesn't suit you."

I say nothing and his face assumes a pleasured calm as he calculates his next verbal attack. When he smiles, I feel dread like a sudden cold drop in my chest.

"Some are homeless," Gavin says, "like your friends in that shelter. I had two of them — requested specially, like a takeaway."

His words feel like blows from a baseball bat wrapped in barbed wire. My blood is loud and I stagger, as if the ground has become unstable.

"Why, Gavin?"

"Because of my unique metabolism."

"Unique... metabolism?"

"Look at me, Gig. Other than the fact I'm not as pretty as you, what do you see?"

With effort, I focus on him.

"You seem to vibrate," I say, "as if you exist at a higher frequency than other people."

"Correct! And why do you suppose that is?"

I think about the hyperspace chamber: time going at a different speed.

"You move faster than everyone else."

"Indeed I do," Gavin says. "In fact, I fit a month's living into twelve hours."

I recall the chequer-plate floor, the steel desks.

"That's why the chamber and the keyboards are made of metal," I say. "Moving that fast, you'd break anything else."

"Now you're getting it."

"And a month in twelve hours is why you've got so many monitors."

"Yes; one system is not enough. I need enormous input to make and issue my decisions. Fortunately, I can type on two keyboards at once, belt out a novel's worth of text in a minute and plan instructions to be carried out over the next thirty-odd days with an average error variance of just 8%."

For some reason, his list of actions terrifies me; but I can't help myself asking, "Why thirty days?"

"It's necessary," Gavin says. "Outside that twelve-hour period once a month, I'm not there to manage it all."

Again, his words have a physical effect: I'm short of breath; the maze appears to close in and the moon looks like a blade about to fall.

"How come you're not there to manage it?" I whisper.

He smiles.

"Because I'm you, Gig."

His words take the last of my strength and I fall backwards, glimpsing the top of the maze, a clear night sky and the stars. The impact should hurt, but shock has robbed my senses.

Gavin steps into view and looks down at my face. "Gig," he says, "every full moon, you turn into me."

You Must Be Joking

I wake up on my side in the roots of a large tree. Party aromas drifting on the warm night air and music flattened by distance tell me it is still Halloween at the Academy.

The earth smells good; rich and woody, overlaid with the iron tang of nearby water. Through the trees a lake shines, surrounding the island like a thick ring of silver in the moonlight. The stars are in a different position to the last time I saw them, so a couple of hours have passed since...

I can't be Gavin; he was standing there talking to me. The whole point of a traditional werewolf transformation is that it's one person in a different state, not separate individuals who can speak to each other. I don't even remember when the moon was full over the last ten years.

Admittedly, I sometimes get more tired than usual and go to sleep early, alone.

Roughly once a month in an Orchard property, where I won't be disturbed.

Above a convenient hyperspace chamber.

I always thought the reason for my strength was to deal with constant pressure, but I must be close to breaking if Gavin can convince me of something so ridiculous. Perhaps the Beanstalk will be my last launch.

And yet, I am a werewolf with impeccable taste and

manners, living in twenty first century England. Does the concept of absurdity even exist anymore?

A block of light illuminates the lower canopy of a tree.

"Gig?"

Helen's voice echoes out of the stairway beneath a hatch.

"Gig, are you all right?"

She steps up and out of the light, becoming a sleek shadow. I raise a hand; she turns and sees me.

"I had to go through the security footage to find you," she says.

"Sorry," I mumble.

"Don't be; it was worth it to see you jump from the shore to the island."

The harsh, artificial light disappears as Helen shuts the door. She picks her way in high heels across the loamy soil and sits with her hip against my shoulder.

"This is the first time you're not the life and soul of the party, Gig," she says. "Don't go getting old on us. The economy is relying on your continued existence."

I want to tell Helen everything, but only manage a grunt as tears blur my view of her.

"Becky came back," Helen says. "She was boggle-eyed with rage because you hadn't gone and found her. I had to get Royal Protection to keep that princess on the other side of the park in case... God, can you imagine?" She laughs. "What a nightmare Becky is."

"Helen rather loves Becky, underneath it all," Gavin says.

I jump up so fast Helen screams and falls backwards.

Gavin stands under a tree four metres away, his face in shadow.

"Gig!" Helen shouts.

"It's all right, Helen," I say, my voice pitched high with tension.

"Gig, what is it?" Helen says.

"Over there," I say and point at Gavin.

Helen shakes as she turns to face the darkness under the trees.

"What?" she says.

She is looking right at Gavin.

I try to speak; can't.

"Shall I come further into the light?" Gavin says.

As he walks forward, I move between him and Helen.

"Gig, what are you doing?" Helen says.

I want to tell her I am protecting her, but again my voice will not work.

"Out of my way, you giant walking carpet," she says, then: "Sorry. I always wanted to say that."

She ducks around and looks up at me.

"Can't you see?" I manage.

She frowns; I point at Gavin again. He is closer now, although I didn't notice him move.

"There," I say. "Right there."

Gavin winces.

"This is going to be awkward," he says.

"I'm sorry, Helen," I gabble. "I don't know how he got in here. I could have killed him but didn't. I can't, people think I can, but I can't."

Helen looks more sad than frightened.

"Kill who, Gig?" she says.

"Gavin Dergs!" I shout.

Helen looks right at Gavin, then back at me.

"I don't understand," Helen says.

"Can't you see him?" I say.

"No," Helen says.

"If she could see me, there'd be more screaming," Gavin says.

"SHUT UP!" I roar at Gavin.

He holds up placating hands, then points at Helen.

She has backed away from me.

"No," I say, "Helen, I…"

"What was that, Gig?" Helen whispers.

I look at Gavin, who wears the expression of a disappointed teacher: it's yourself you've let down, Gig.

I shake my head.

"Nothing," I say. "I've just been under a lot of pressure."

"'Under a lot of pressure?'" Gavin says. "You sound like a wife-beater."

He laughs, but Helen still doesn't see him.

"I'm going to go," she says.

It's as if she has struck me.

"No," I say, "please don't."

"It's best if she does," Gavin says.

"Helen?" I say, aware of my pleading tone.

"God, this is painful," Gavin says.

He strides over and waves his hands in Helen's face.

"Hello!" Gavin shouts. "Hello, Helen!"

Gavin turns to me, and shrugs.

"She can't see me, Gig," Gavin says. "Why do you suppose that is?"

"Gig," Helen says, "what do you keep looking at?"

"Yes, Gig," Gavin joins in. "What?"

He touches Helen's hair, but the hair does not move. He touches her dress, but there is no indentation where his fingers land.

"Okay, Helen, best you go," I say.

Gavin's hand stops moving, his gaze fixed on my eyes.

"I'm not feeling well," I say, "but I'll be okay soon. See you back with the others."

It hurts to see how fast Helen walks back to the hatch, leaving it to slam shut behind her.

For a moment, there is no sound or movement, as if I am trapped in a picture.

"Phew," Gavin says. "Even I found that uncomfortable. Still, you could do better: all these years and she never figured out Gig Danvers and Gavin Dergs are anagrams of each other. Tut tut."

"How are you doing this?" I say.

He smiles.

"It took me years to reach you," he says. "No end of experiment, injection and goodness knows what else. Exceptionally painful, I might add."

I watch him.

"Hm, no pity for your old mate Gav," he continues, "but that's fine. Most of the time I existed in one hyperspace chamber or another, channelling the world via computers. Then I found a way to shadow you, and then worked out how to break through.

"It's the moon, you see. It's with us nearly all the time, even during the day. While I don't become you like I do when the moon is full, I can engage with you like this, using the moon in its lesser form."

"But how are you engaging with me?" I say.

"A combination of frequency and tolerance," Gavin says. "I don't just move fast to concentrate a month into twelve hours, I actually live that month, which creates a unique temporal structure. The chronological frequency is thus a series of wavelengths whose tips can, and do, touch. It's delicate, though, and involves quantum-level connections which are hard to predict and manipulate. That's where tolerance comes in."

"Ironic," I say, "considering your politics."

"Different kind of tolerance, Gig. It's like the way I operate through four human directors. They have a broad remit to do what they want, providing those decisions ultimately align with my plan. I give each director a set of instructions to complete every month. They either carry out those instructions or present reasons why not, which I then factor into the next month."

"That sounds… enlightened," I say.

"Of course it's enlightened," Gavin says. "Mind you, I have killed a few directors, which the current ones know about. I also only hire people with families, for hostage purposes."

I didn't think I could feel any sicker.

"So," Gavin says, "tolerance. It's the same as my interactions with you. This conversation is my estimate of what we are both likely to say, informed by infinitesimal connections that make your Beanstalk technology look like the hack job it is."

"How can I see you?" I say. "How can I hear you?"

"I'm part of you, remember?" Gavin says. "An aspect so deeply hidden you don't even know it's there. All I have to do is reach through, engage with your senses and here we are."

I put my head my hands. My fur and the shape of my skull feel unfamiliar, as if they belong to someone else.

When I look up, Gavin is still there. I sigh.

"This plan you mentioned," I say. "What is it?"

For the first time, Gavin doesn't look revolting; instead, his face is eager. He reaches for me and I feel his grip, even though the fur on my arm does not move.

"There is a Wall between us and where we came from," Gavin says.

I stare at him.

"Ten years ago, you and I just occurred," Gavin goes on. "How? What are we, really? What are we meant to do?"

"Not kill people," I say.

Gavin lets go of my arm and his habitual sneer returns.

"You waste your time fixing things these idiot monkeys could have sorted out decades ago," he says. "They don't deserve it."

"They do."

"Gig, we have to break through that Wall."

"No."

"I know we can do it," Gavin says. "Look at the miracle of us speaking now!"

"Miracle is not the word I'd use."

Gavin snorts, then gets himself under control.

"We are not of this world," he says. "You're too good; I'm too bad – even I know that."

He stares up into the night sky.

"I doubt we were meant to be split at all, Gig. It was probably an accident, like a teleport beam going wrong –"

"A teleport beam?"

He looks at me again.

"Well, whatever. But…"

Gavin seems to run out of breath, and inhales deeply.

"We have to know," he says.

"I'd rather we focus on you not being a fascist."

Gavin's face tightens with frustration.

"The Nazi crap is a way to get what I need," he says, "before it's too late."

I regard him.

"The water wars you talked about," I say.

"The water wars are only part of it. Soon, people with resources will be using them just to exist. Everyone else…"

He surprises me by looking sad.

"There'll be no industry, no infrastructure, no research," he says. "No way to get through the Wall and break free."

"You could be free now."

"No, I can't; I tried. Moving fast isn't a choice for me; I don't get to speed up just when it's convenient, any more than you can stop being a werewolf. We're both like it all the time. I nearly died more than once hitting the side of a table, shattering my hand and nearly bleeding out. If it wasn't for your healing abilities, we'd both be dead.

"I can't speak to anyone; they barely see me, and my voice is so fast it's incomprehensible. I can't touch them: they burst like ripe fruit and all I can do is devour them. The only person I can talk to is you, which brings its own complications, does it not?"

Remembering those marks on the walls of the hyperspace chamber, I imagine the rage that propelled objects to savage that metal so deeply. As I try and fail to find the right words, Gavin puts his hands on my shoulders and looks in my eyes.

"You'll end up ruler of what's left of the world," he says, "while I carry on suffocating in a steel box."

He shakes his head.

"I will never let that happen, Gig. Never."

Gavin lets go and walks away, into the green and orange light.

Paranormal Activity

I've never seen myself sleep before.

In Gavin's emailed recording, I lie curled on a large bed. There is no sheet covering me, and I'm alone. The luxurious room has floor-to-ceiling windows, through which glowing clouds part to reveal a full moon.

The video arrived just now. Its O5 stamp confirms its legitimacy, not that anyone would think to invent anything this insane.

I click on pause and glance up to check I'm still alone. There is no one else in the office at 9.30pm; nothing to keep me from this unwanted revelation.

I unfreeze the recording.

Moonlight catches my sleeping outline, sketching me in silver. I begin to glow, and realise my fur absorbs moonlight as well as sunshine.

The superstring wasn't the first Product derived from my fur; the solar battery was, although we kept it quiet to encourage other renewable research. Notionally vegan, I am 60% solar-powered and can retain energy for long periods, even in darkness. The process I am witnessing appears to follow the same principles, but in a frightful new direction.

In the recording, my fur begins to vibrate as if it's being pulled out. I roll onto my knees, then flip over as if the bed has become electrified. I flail and twitch: eyes open, but black and sightless. Head thrashing and teeth bared, I shake as if the moonlit room has become freezing. My fur blazes white and becomes translucent, revealing black skin that ripples as though huge worms are writhing beneath it. The fur stabs back in, bringing whiteness to my flesh that spreads like a stain.

I go to increase the volume and see it's at maximum. Even my screams are silent.

My limbs contract as if they are telescopic and being forced back to their minimum position. My snout recedes like the tip is being hit with a sledgehammer. Soon I become a pale streak: hairless, with wide black eyes and a gash for a mouth. The teeth are sharper than a normal person's, the nails long.

Gavin Dergs stares up into the camera right at me, then the bed shunts aside to reveal a floor hatch that opens so quickly it's as if a rectangle of floor has turned black. Gavin disappears through the hatch; it closes after him and the bed slides back into place.

The recording stops on the image of that empty, motionless bed. As I struggle to process what I have just seen, the email deletes itself. With slow fingers and a slower mind, I search my computer system.

There's no trace of the email, or the recording.

When I first appeared, the Security Services experimented by shooting me with a mortar. The missile hit my head, and for a moment all I knew was horrible clanging nausea that felt like it was boiling out of my ears.

This feels like that.

I look at the time and date on my screen. The next full moon is tomorrow.

And So, Farewell

It's later the same night and the Orchard helicopter that dropped me near the border with the Welsh Protectorate clatters off into the dark. We have a distribution centre near Hereford, so I have a reason for this last-minute journey, although by the time anyone finds out where I've gone it will be too late.

The dread moon is hidden behind thick cloud. It's quiet and there is little life here, just dry grass. Even the foxes have gone.

To the west, grids of light hack into the darkened countryside as towns and cities join to form one vast urban sprawl out of London. There is little movement on those distant roads, but it is late now: around 1.30am.

To the east, a rough assembly of barbed wire, half-built brick barriers and tumbled earth forms a jagged line against the dull sky. Cheaper than the ten-metre-high statement wall that separates the Kingdom of England from the Northern Republic, this one is less effective too. It's just as well; the only planes flying to the US go from the Welsh Protectorate, and I have discovered a cargo flight leaving in two hours.

Gripping the Skywolf, I activate the invisibility hormone and dash across the stubbly ground. I can't hear or smell anyone as I approach the border; it seems to be automated.

Not many people want to get into the Welsh Protectorate, and the number trying to leave has fallen sharply in recent years. Nobody knows why.

Springing from the embankment, I soar in the warm air and the barrier appears to swing like a door below me. On the far side, I hit the ground and run towards a clump of dark buildings half a kilometre away. An alarm sounds and a searchlight clacks on, sweeping the ground five metres ahead. I shoot out the searchlight and reel in the Skywolf cable as I head back to the border.

I'm still almost invisible, so when the sound of booted feet gets louder I wait motionless near an abandoned truck. Ten guards whose shapes are rough in the darkness examine the vehicle. Finding nothing, they head south along the border and I follow them. If I can keep close, I should convince the boundary scanners I'm part of the patrol.

The guards talk in panicky tones as they search, scared about getting into trouble because they've let someone in. Strangely, none of them speak with a Welsh accent and they aren't American either; they're English.

The guards split into two groups; I follow those heading in the direction of the coast and lose them amid silent, empty buildings. After that, I lope through unkempt fields and deserted roads, then...

Wait, what's this?

I'm in the middle of a town. The streetlamps are off; the houses dark and empty with curtains open despite the hour. None of their windows or those of the cars parked along kerbs or in driveways are broken. No rubbish is blown by the hot night wind; there aren't even any dogs barking.

A distant searchlight illuminates the road and I see my shadow. My exertions have made me visible, but no one comes out to challenge me.

I set off again, sprinting into the darkness towards Cardiff.

I find other towns and villages like the first; battened down as if waiting for something. Much of the country is dark; not through lack of electricity – the Beanstalk now beams down plenty – but because everything is switched off.

Cardiff is livelier, but only just. Some of the roads are lit; there are even a few cars moving along them. However, the view is like a sketch of the Welsh capital rather than the illuminated city it should be.

I pause in the darkness, kneel and press my hands onto spiky grass that feels new-grown. An out-of-town shopping or cinema complex must have stood here; gone now, along with its inhabitants, leaving only a strange vibration in the ground.

There's no time to investigate and, besides, what secret is greater than the one I carry? Cardiff airport is still thirty minutes away, so I ignore the trembling earth and race on.

I run through alleys, over roofs, and fire the Skywolf at an office tower. Swinging high over the city centre, I land on the far side, then head through silent industrial estates and darkened suburbs until I reach the airport.

At the perimeter, I expect more searchlights and alarms; but when I leap the outer fence, nothing happens. Easing around the airport boundary, I spot my plane: a huge old Antonov. Blocky grey containers are lifted into the cargo bay, after which the undercarriage doors shut.

This is it: my last night on Earth. I never even said goodbye to Becky.

The hum in the ground is displaced by the Antonov's engines as it taxis into position. It's the only plane moving; the others are parked like those cars in the towns.

I enable the chameleon hormone, unsling the Skywolf and run after the plane. It goes fast for such a monster, and I speed up when the great wheel racks leave the ground. Closing in as the Antonov lumbers into the air, I fire the little suction pad at the vehicle's underside. Still running, I activate the motor and then I'm airborne too, carried up into darkness above the half-conscious city.

Soon we're over the pale-streaked gloom of the Atlantic, with United Ireland a bright patch to my right. I just need to maintain my grip on the Skywolf for another four hours and then…

Even if the fall doesn't kill me, I will be further from anywhere I can swim to before I turn into Gavin. He won't survive the cold or the currents, and maintaining his extraordinary speed will exhaust him far from land.

My existence ends at the same time. The Kingdom of England must find another Royal Protector, another unlikely resource to peg its currency to. I wonder if they'll keep the L.

The plane is no longer visible; it's flying too high for me to breathe, so I extend the superstring and soar above the ocean. Buffeted by velocity and air currents, I focus less on fate and responsibility than the simple need to hang on.

Oh, Becky I don't want to do this. I wish I could see you again, but can think of no other way out. I considered a retreat from everything to hide on an island with you somewhere, but how can I escape Gavin?

I thought I was doing good; that most traditional route to atrocity. Instead, I have balanced every achievement with its exact opposite. I shudder as I imagine more Beanstalks growing around the world, controlled by Gavin's creepy, fanatical associates.

These things might come to pass anyway; perhaps all I've done is delay the inevitable. However, it's absurd to imagine that a single person can affect any kind of salvation. It is particularly inaccurate in my case, not just because Gavin has weaponised my Products but because I rely on Becky and Helen completely, as well as everyone who works for Orchard. For too long and despite our efforts, the myth persists that there is a Special One and that it's me.

So, to prevent anyone interpreting my disappearance and Gavin's as anything mysterious or divine, I have left Becky and Helen a message with a time delay set for twenty-four hours. The video is verifiably genuine and details the truth, as much as I understand it.

Becky and Helen will have final say about whether the Beanstalk stays up or is destroyed. The same process that enlarged the cables can be used to diminish them from the ground up, with the orbital anchor cut adrift before detonating.

The lit clock on the Skywolf tells me I have already been airborne for fifty-eight minutes.

I've got three hours left.

Three hours later

Just a few more minutes?

Twenty minutes later

I fumble with the controls and begin ascending towards the plane. If I pass out then it won't be a conscious decision to let go, which I have convinced myself will be easier.

The Skywolf motor gets me up faster than I wanted, however. Already I can see the plane, its lights a red smudge in the high, thin air.

My lungs begin to strain and cold seeps into my fur. Not long now –

I'm falling!

How –?

Spinning in the dark, I hurl the Skywolf away. The sea is a whisper getting louder as its briny scent overwhelms me. Wind blasts my face, bringing the taste of far-off deserts and jungles amid the vast cold sweep of ocean with its giant, symphonic echoes.

I tumble head over heels until the heaving surface is right there: its foamy details nothing out of the ordinary, except for my position in relation to them.

Becky –?

Bad Boy

Gavin sits by the bed, his expression as close to sympathetic as he can manage. It's day, and through a window I see the gleaming strip of the southeast Beanstalk cable. Little else is visible: indifferent clouds trundle across a grey sky and a safety beacon somewhere below casts pulsing orange luminescence against the metal window frame.

I'm on the launch platform, which is now twenty times bigger to accommodate the new spaceport. The rocket far above has grown as well; the same size as the platform, it nestles at the heart of an array of gigantic solar collectors. On clear days, you can see it; although knowing it's connected to the ground is disorienting, and vertigo becomes even more intense when I picture someone heading up there in a capsule.

I thought the first person to travel up the Beanstalk would be me. Last night I accepted it would be someone else: Becky, maybe, with Helen. Now it looks as if it might be me again, the prospect no longer inspires.

Indeed, I'm not sure how I feel about anything. Suicide is so alien to me I have no idea how to process my attempt. Maybe I'll never be able to, and the memory will drift outside me like the Beanstalk anchor.

"You'll be wondering how I pulled this off," Gavin says.

"No," I say.

"Not now, perhaps, as you're having a bit of a moment, but soon. Time is short, as well as restricted in other ways, so I'll tell you –"

"Don't bother."

"Gig, you need to know so you can do something about it."

"Go away."

Gavin stares at me.

"Gig," he says, "either I tell you so you put measures in place that drive my operation to ever more inventive ways of thwarting you; or you lie there like a rug and I do it all again.

"Now then, I'm going to start. If at any point you want me to stop, just wave a paw."

I don't move.

"Super!" Gavin says. "First, we've got the organic computer and we've got hux as well."

"I accepted that would happen, eventually," I say.

"And you don't mind," Gavin says, "because Products 5 and 6 thwart extremism by engendering a truly empathetic world view, as you found out after that stunt with Saxon Jihad."

He smiles.

"See?" he says. "I really am a fan."

I feel like a giant, invisible hand is crushing me.

"You stole Wales," I say.

Gavin looks out of the window, then back at me.

"Borrowed, technically," he says. "But as I have no intention of giving it back: yes. That's a chat for another time. For now, you need to understand how easy it is to manipulate data in the O5 space."

"The whole point is that you manipulate data in the O5 space," I say.

"I mean manipulate it at a very basic level," Gavin says. "So: I sent you footage of your transformation into me, because until then you secretly thought this whole thing was a con and I wasn't really you at all. Yes?"

I glare at him, then nod.

"You had less than a day to do something," Gavin continues, "and there was really only one solution: arrange to die when you were me. It's what I'd have done."

He waits for me to react, but I just watch him. His eyes narrow.

"Our monthly transformation took place the night before I sent you the footage," Gavin says. "I altered the Orchard system to change the date."

Breathing is a sudden problem, as is the dreadful ache in my heart.

Gavin smiles.

"It's the same method I used to delete your little confession," he says. "That's the trouble when you stop talking to people, Gig. You end up relying on automated communication, while basic things like the date go right out of the window."

I resist the urge to hug myself.

"I do talk to people," I say.

"Less and less," Gavin says. "You haven't seen Helen for weeks, and even dear Becky's had the cold shoulder."

He's right. It's as if the idea of my friends is now more attractive than the reality of being with them.

I don't understand why, though.

"I've had a tracker on you for years," Gavin says. "It's in that mouthpiece in your tooth. You should get rid of it if you don't want me to know where you are.

"The plane was mine, by the way. My people detached the Skywolf by cutting the sucker out of the fuselage from inside, in case you hoisted yourself to a height even you couldn't survive falling from. Those Antonov sky buses were designed to launch space planes, so it was easy to adapt one to carry the small chopper that was used to pick you up. Then you were dropped back here. No one even noticed you were gone."

I wish he would get to the end, so I can sleep again.

"Anyway," he says, "I can see it's all been a bit much, so I'll leave you with this thought: even though I stopped you killing me, I'm still angry that you tried. There have been consequences. There will always be consequences."

He picks the remote up from the bedside table and turns on the television. It is set to a news channel, and an image so awful I can't understand it at first.

The top left of the screen shows a map with a road marked in red. Under the map is the familiar upside-down A representing Thera and the new currency. Live footage on the right shows a giant version of the same symbol built from semi-transparent material rising from some grotty shrubs by the side of a road. Fixed to the symbol is a man covered in blood, his hair thick with it.

Fire officers try to cut him free; however, he has been attached with superstring. They can't get through the structure holding him either, because it is made of a similar substance to my claws. Paramedics try to bring the man back to life: his body jerks as they apply defibrillator paddles to his chest, but it's no good.

Otis is dead, crucified behind a service station on the A3.

Disclosure

Helen shoots most of an entire clip at me before dropping the assault rifle and saying, "This just isn't working."

Behind her, Becky is all huge eyes and thick hair she's pulled in every direction.

"I mean," Helen goes on and she's doing that laughing/crying thing that's so awful, "it's not like it was actually you, is it?"

I told them the day after we scattered Otis's ashes over the field around the temple with ten thousand people in attendance. A day after that the three of us are in Orchard Academy's huge atmospheric test chamber.

"It wasn't," I say, "and at the same time, it was."

Becky groans. Helen snatches up the assault rifle and points it at her.

"Throw up again," Helen says to Becky. "I dare you."

"Helen," I say.

Helen doesn't take her eyes off Becky.

"We need her," I say.

"Hm," Helen says.

"He picked up the remote, you see," I say.

They both turn.

"Remote?" Becky says.

"I hadn't thought about it before now," I say, "but...

Gavin picked up the remote and used it to turn on the telly."

"Shit," Becky says.

"Gavin used a remote control," Helen says. "So what?"

Shock has made her slow.

"He wasn't really there," I say. "When he talks to me he's some kind of projection. He shouldn't have been able to do anything."

Helen puts the assault rifle on the floor and shoves it away with her foot.

"Gavin Dergs has figured out how to manipulate me, even when it's not a full moon. He does it in such a way that my actions look like his."

Becky's hands shake as she smooths her hair back down.

"We have to assume," she says, "that Gavin will soon be able to take you over completely."

"Yes," I say.

"And we can't kill you because it isn't possible," Helen says.

I go to apologise and stop myself in time.

"If we try and get Gavin," Helen continues, "his people will murder us the way they did Otis."

"Yes," I say.

"Plus the Kingdom's economy is pegged to you, Gig," Becky says. "The only thing holding the country together is money; take that away and…"

For a while, we stand in the great empty space.

"I did have one idea," I say.

Helen looks at Becky, who shrugs.

"Let's hear it, then," Becky says. "Neither of us has a clue."

"Go through the Wall," I say.

"This mythical boundary separating you from where you came from?" Helen says.

"Yes," I say.

Helen shakes her head.

"I refuse to give Gavin Dergs what he wants," she says.

"What if he's right?" I say.

"How can he be right?" Becky says.

"Evil is not a calculation for him," I say. "It's simply how he is."

Helen looks at the assault rifle again.

"How can we be sure it's Gig and not Gavin saying this?" she says.

I go to deny it, and then say, "I don't know."

"Gig," Becky says, "there has been so much change already; more than people can cope with."

"People can cope with change," I say, "as long as it's managed properly, as long as it's fair and as long as they know what's going on. You of all people should know that, Becky."

"I'm tired," Becky says. "Burned out, in fact."

"No you're not," I tell her.

Even as I say it, I notice the lines on Becky's face; that all her hair is grey, while her right hand trembles as if planning an escape. Helen has a strange smile: it's almost lopsided. I realise she cakes on more makeup these days; that the unchanging hair is a wig now. Both my friends have aged as I ... just carry on.

"I don't want a life without both of you," I say. "Selfish, I know, but it's bad enough Otis has gone. I'll outlast you both easily, and others like you and I... I don't want that."

"But you love everyone, Gig," Becky says.

The walls feel as if they're spinning. Dizzy and sick, I try to find a focus that isn't Becky or Helen. Concentrating intensifies the nausea, so I stand there until things calm down, or seem to. I hope for some optimistic solution; but instead say, "You're forgetting Gavin. He's been trying to take me over since I arrived."

Air in the test chamber seems close, despite the size of the room. It emphasises the silence: the only sound comes from their hearts beating; Helen's faster than Becky's. Helen shakes her head and I expect her to walk out.

"How do we even start?" she says, surprising me as she always does. "This Wall Gavin wants to break through is so theoretical I…"

She turns to Becky, who gazes at the floor as if there's an answer there, albeit one she can't understand.

"You want to break through something we can't even perceive," Becky says.

"We know it involves the moon," I say.

"Does it, though?" Becky says, looking up. "The moon could just symbolise something else."

"It's a start," Helen says. "So the moon was most likely formed when a comet hit the Earth in its early days. Now it orbits us –"

"No," Becky says. "Earth and moon orbit each other around a central point called the barycentre. If the Earth and moon were the same size, the barycentre would be between them and they'd circle around it.

"But the moon is much smaller, so the barycentre is within the Earth itself. It's…" her eyes widen, "a two-body problem." She giggles, that blue look in her eyes. "Literally in your case."

"Oh, she's good," Gavin says from my left. "I see why you love her so."

Becky and Helen stare at me. I sigh.

"He's here," I say, and point: the tip of my index claw stopping at Gavin's temple.

Becky and Helen's eyes click over and it's almost as if they can see Gavin. I look at them, then at him. His black eyes are bleak, his sneer half-hearted.

"Yeah," he says.

Helen picks up the assault rifle again.

"That won't work," I say.

Helen stretches her arms to point the barrel at herself.

"Yes, it will," she says.

"Helen –" Becky begins.

"This is what you made me want to do!" Helen screams at Gavin. "Are you happy now?"

Gavin's face is without expression as he slowly shakes his head.

"He's shaking his head," I shout at Helen, desperate for her to put the weapon down.

She doesn't seem to hear.

"Becky can talk all she wants about two-body problems," Helen says. "She can talk about abstract realms made real by altering our minds, but the true physics are these: the only way out of this situation is for the four of us here now to work together. And I can't do that."

"Don't do it for him," I say, "do it for us."

"No!" Helen says.

Becky is shaking as she stares at the assault rifle.

"For the Kingdom, then," she says.

Helen's nostrils flare.

"However much you give the Kingdom," Helen says, "it will always take more."

"Yes," Gavin says, "but there is a way around that."

I repeat his words to Helen.

"Oh," Helen says, "are we in agreement now, Gavin?"

Gavin goes to speak, but hesitates; his mouth opens and closes as if he's rehearsing for something.

"Um…" he says.

I glare at Gavin.

"She is holding an assault rifle to her head," I remind him.

Gavin nods furiously. Where is his trademark psycho patter when I need it most? I remember then how he's never spoken to anyone, except me.

Fortunately, Gavin recalls what he wanted to say.

"If we can reconcile this, now, we can reconcile anything," he says and I keep my voice flat to differentiate his words from mine, "from the political chaos to the impossibility that is me and Gig."

Helen's arms tremble with the weight of the rifle, and she leans her upper body forward to accommodate it.

"Is that why you did it all, then?" Helen says.

"I don't know," Gavin says. "Probably."

As I relay Gavin's answer, Helen's eyelids flicker. She looks like she is trying to disconnect from the situation, without moving.

"Helen," Becky says.

"No, Becky," Helen says. "I don't know how I, or any of us, can do this."

"There was never an instruction manual," Becky says, "for…"

She gestures to me.

"It's about negotiating freedoms," Gavin says and again I repeat his words. "Put down the weapon and I will explain how your entire life has led to this point."

Helen hurls the assault rifle at Gavin and it passes through him. Helen's face begins to shake as if she's having a seizure. Becky steps up behind Helen and injects her neck with something; then catches her as she sags to the floor.

Through it all, Gavin watches Becky with an even stranger expression than usual.

From Celebrity Werewolf:
The Biography of Gig Danvers
By Andrew Wallace

The murder of Otis Pyke-Jones galvanised the Kingdom's many opposing forces. The predations of extremist political parties had not been forgotten, and neither had the manipulations of the aristocracy. Many people saw their new wealth as a means of taking revenge, while heavily armed nationalists looked forward to commencing a conflict they had wanted for decades.

Otis's crucifixion should have brought about this long-dreaded civil war; however, a week after his cremation he began to appear around the Kingdom.

Surveillance confirmed the resurrections were genuine. In addition, people described Otis touching their hands and speaking to them, although his conversation involved writing advice rather than descriptions of the afterlife.

Otis would walk into a pub or living room, and was always dressed the same: in his mummy outfit minus the headpiece. He displayed no injuries or scars and seemed unaware that he was, or had been, dead. At the end of each encounter he would leave, although attempts at pursuit or subsequent contact proved unsuccessful.

People suspected a trick, but not for long. Emergency service reports from the scene of Otis's murder were made public, while no one who saw the tremulous public statements made by the police officers and paramedics who attended could doubt their sincerity.

Gig Danvers himself was proof that the uncanny could exist alongside the ordinary, although even after the tenth resurrection of Otis Pyke-Jones no one at Orchard was available for comment.

Homework

Much of Helen's physicality is charisma and rage; she appears smaller without them as she lies unconscious in a hospital bed. She wears an off-white smock the same colour as her patchy hair. It doesn't suit her any more than the unfamiliar repose, in which her lovely face is so lined it looks soft.

We are in one of Orchard Academy's medical suites. The floor of the large, pale yellow room is terracotta resin, which echoes an occasional soft beep from one of the machines. The bed is central, its headboard against the wall opposite a window whose blinds are drawn against another hot, dry night. The air conditioning keeps us comfortable, but it's working harder than usual because of the research equipment we have installed in here.

Becky sits at a table next to the bed. Her long, grey hair is slicked back tight against her head and then braided: the neatest I've ever seen it. Wearing nothing except the shirt she put on three days earlier she hasn't slept, although her eyes are bright. She has been dividing her time between looking after Helen and working with me to figure out how to get through the Wall.

We have directed every Orchard resource to the problem, using an O5 network so powerful that our monitors reveal an entirely new kind of data. This informational paradigm has inspired Becky to forget her loathing of computers, and she hammers on her keyboard as if it's an old typewriter.

Gavin sits on a chair by the window. He does not move and only speaks to direct us.

We are at work on a new set of metrics. They include physical samples and highly detailed analyses of Gavin, because while Becky and I spent ten years deriving advantages from my physical being, Gavin has used the time to study himself.

We examine the ways he produces energy, and I begin to understand what his body and brain do to manage that exceptional speed. There are psychological studies as well, which reveal how Gavin's narcissism is rooted less in his physical aspect than the love he has for his own mind.

The presence of Gavin has not affected Becky's sexual appetite. Her reduced stamina is compensated for by a muscular focus that prevents energy being expended on anything except the lush, tight path to orgasm.

Tonight, while her hands move over me and I feel her essence tremble and clench, her eyes are fixed on where she knows Gavin's are. He does not move, and looks right back at her.

As usual, I lose awareness when I climax with Becky but even so I notice Gavin shake like he's been punched in the gut, his mouth wide and eyes closed. I think at first it is pleasure or pain, but then I see his black eyes are wet.

For a while I hold Becky, and then she hauls herself off me to stand dripping in front of Gavin. I imagine Becky's powerful mind constructing Gavin so thoroughly she can see him, almost as clearly as I can.

"Your physicality is misplaced," Becky says to Gavin. "The werewolf is supposed to be the monster, not the man. A two-body problem..."

She steps back to the monitors, pulling the shirt over her gleaming skin. I join her.

"Orbits," she says. "Gravity: time and space…"

"The Otis resurrections," I say.

"They are…" Becky begins.

"Manifestations of a phenomenon that has not yet occurred," Gavin says. "We know we will break through the Wall, because in one dimension it's already happened. Do you see, now?"

"Yes," Helen says from the bed.

We turn to her.

"You can hear him?" I say.

"I can," Helen says.

Gavin jumps up, his eyes shining.

"Can you… see me?" he says, his voice high, like a boy's.

"Yes, Gavin," Helen says. "I can see you."

"I can't," Becky mutters, but only I hear.

"Helen!" Gavin says. "Helen!"

Helen sits up, her face unreadable.

"Yes, Gavin."

Gavin stares at Helen as if she is the most beautiful thing he has ever seen.

"It's just…" Gavin says, tears falling from his black eyes. "I've never spoken to anyone else before. Not properly. And… I shouldn't… be able… to talk to you now. I mean I'm not here. I'm not… I never imagined this would happen. How is it possible?"

Helen gets up and stands on the polished floor by the bed.

"Everything is so bright," she says, "as if illumination is coming out of me in beams of silver and gold. You're in it, Gavin; you and Gig."

Gavin's expression is beatific. He takes a step closer to Helen, and then the horror of all he has done hits him, revealed like celestial wrath. His face vibrates; he looks like he's in a centrifuge as memories of atrocity shake his flesh. He tries to cross the room to Helen, but moves through an impossible reality that rushes against him like a torrent.

Still he reaches for Helen, knuckles cracking as he fights to extend his fingers. He looks runty beside her, though, and must know she will knock him aside.

Instead, Helen steps up to Gavin and holds him. Whatever force prevented Gavin from reaching Helen fades and Gavin stands there, arms by his sides as if he has no idea what else to do with them.

"Oh," he says.

Being a werewolf, I'm accustomed to expressions of instinctive disbelief; but nothing I've experienced captures the essence of astonishment quite like that gasping croak of Gavin's.

Helen is still connected to the life-signs monitor, which starts to behave strangely.

"Helen," Becky says, "whatever you're doing, you need to stop."

Becky goes towards Helen, but something prevents her getting closer. Becky looks surprised, as if her limbs have refused to obey her.

The monitor sounds an alarm.

"Helen!" Becky's voice is a shriek now.

Gavin looks up into Helen's face. She smiles and he touches her cheek with a trembling hand.

"There's so much I have to tell you," Gavin says.

"I know," Helen says.

Like Becky, I'm unable to move; fixed into this seemingly banal scene: a woman embracing a man; another woman nearby; a werewolf everyone has got used to; a bed; some equipment.

Strange, then, how I feel like the eye of the world.

"I have to go," Helen says.

"What?" Gavin says.

"It must be this way," Helen says. "Not what I wanted,

truly, but still. I –"

She dies.

It is sudden, but not violent. Helen is simply no longer there; all that remains is the body of a dark-skinned woman wearing one of those dresses you only get in hospitals, hooked up to some beeping machines.

Becky falls to her knees as Helen slides to the floor.

"No!" Becky screams, "*No!*"

Able to move again, she crawls to Helen and holds her as doctors run in. One of them calls for assistance; Becky will not let go of Helen and has to be sedated.

Gavin's face is blank as he silently weeps, unable to believe his connection with humanity has been taken from him at the very instant he found it. He begins to fade as the moon moves out of reach, hidden in the sky on the other side of the world.

For one last moment, we are all together. Then he is gone, Helen is gone, Becky is away from me and I am alone again.

From Celebrity Werewolf:
The Biography of Gig Danvers
By Andrew Wallace

To understand how everyone discovered that Gig Danvers and Gavin Dergs were the same individual, we must return to Wales.

By now, the Protectorate's super-churches had become heavily fortified, decadent palaces whose congregations were virtual. Gavin Dergs was therefore able to infiltrate information feeds trusted by the evangelicals to tell them what they wanted to hear, rather than the truth.

Dergs then replaced the religious state police with a commercial version, although use of Orchard Products 5 and 6 meant the usual excesses were avoided. Instead, everyone began working together to turn abandoned mines into a subterranean living intelligence network. More and more people plugged themselves into a system that, far from controlling them, evolved at the same time and in the same way that they did.

The Welsh Protectorate thus became a secret hybrid of human and supercomputer. It had a single goal: establish how to get through 'the Wall' that prevented the werewolf from discovering how he came to be. As part of this process, the

Protectorate analysed samples from both Gig Danvers and Gavin Dergs, quickly realising that what appeared to be divergent DNA was a bizarrely complex reflection of itself.

The resulting political furore was even more extreme than the one that greeted Gig on his arrival. How could the factions of England fight each other when they were represented by the same entity? The looming civil war, which had been the great dread of the age, petered out because for once the pointlessness of such a conflict was recognised before it began, rather than afterwards.

The evangelicals were thrown out; England and Wales formed a new, more powerful union, and the national infrastructure Gig had laboured over was finally implemented. The diverse elements of Britain then joined forces to do two things: find out what was behind that mysterious Wall, and arrest Gig Danvers.

The Journey Home

They get Becky when she goes out for milk one morning.

"I will not eat dry cereal!" she yells, shaking a box of Frosties at me.

Ten minutes after she stomps out of the rented cottage to the village nearby, I hear her over the transmitter Helen used to use.

"I love you, baby," Becky says, and I know she's been taken. "Bye."

We had agreed that if this happened I wouldn't try and rescue her. With the resources of a united Britain at our disposal, we are close to a solution for getting through the Wall.

However, without Helen and Becky I find I care less and less; only determination to make the horror worthwhile keeps me going. I feel heavy, though, as if my bones have increased in mass with no extra strength to carry them.

I leave the cottage and wait in the woods nearby. I've got the invisibility hormone activated and there's a new model Skywolf strapped across my back. Helicopters batter the high air, and the countryside is alive with movement. My mind seems to be doing something similar; ideas and decisions tumble through it, are forgotten, tumble through again.

"Maybe if just I turn myself in, they'll let Becky go," I say.

"We can't predict what will happen," Gavin says. "We're not in charge any more."

He no longer manifests visually and exists as a voice in my head, quiet with intense grief. Fears of me becoming more 'evil' as he becomes more 'good' prove groundless. Instead we find ourselves in a unique state of confusion as we approach the next full moon.

Otis has ceased to appear, as if his afterlife was somehow linked to Helen's earthly one. Meanwhile, the Protectorate has determined that Otis' appearances were not random after all. Totalled up and marked on a map of the Kingdom, they point to the Beanstalk.

A leaf rustles nearby.

"Becky?" I say.

It's not her; just a vole racing through the undergrowth.

Gavin's despair floods me.

"How are you talking to me?" I say, to get his mind off it. "We're way outside your zones of tolerance."

"I think I'm channelling the Protectorate," Gavin says.

Down by the cottage, police officers armed with reciprocating swords and frazzle nets spread out across the field. Khaki vehicles full of soldiers approach along the access road from the south, accompanied by rail guns on robotic four-legged walkers.

"This all looks flatteringly serious," I say.

"Those rail guns will push you onto the reciprocating swords," Gavin says. "The blades are derived from your claws, so there's a good chance they'll get one of your limbs off."

"And the frazzle nets…?"

"Carry an electrical charge that will overwhelm you."

"Right," I say. "Thanks."

The soldiers disembark and join the police as the rail gun walkers get into position.

"Gig," Gavin says. "You have to move."

"I don't think I want to," I say.

"You think I do? When Helen looked at me, spoke to me, t-touched me… I only had moments with her, Gig, but it was like a lifetime. For her, too, I think; it's why she died –"

"Can you comprehend what Helen meant to me, Gavin?"

"Yes! I still feel her, somehow… Gig, it's like she's become God."

There are more troops behind us, close to the northern edge of the wood.

"Gig!"

"Haven't we done enough, Gavin?"

"It doesn't end like this, Gig; or on some vivisection table."

"How do you know?"

"Because Helen shouldn't have been able to see me. Otis shouldn't have come back from the dead. I'm… beginning to understand. There's so much data flowing into me –"

"How?"

"Because Orchard Product 1 was werewolf venom after all."

"It wasn't."

"Your Products use some physical aspect of you, and so do mine. They have been absorbed into humanity."

"Gavin, no one is going to sprout fur and a muzzle."

"No," Gavin says, "but instead they engage with each other and with us in an entirely new way. When I decided to turn the Protectorate into a supercomputer I had in mind the old zombie model, where hackers used a virus to enslave personal computers and create a modular system with huge processing power. I was going to do that with people, then just plug them in whether they liked it or not.

"They embraced it, though, and live in a new realm – probably quantum but not necessarily. And… that's where I exist. I didn't realise before, when I was a monster; but when

Helen touched me everything burst open. At that moment, she knew everything I knew.

"It's how you solve a two-body problem, Gig. You become one body."

The soldiers are in the wood now. Another two rail gun walkers are with them.

"Gavin," I say, "are you asking me to give you complete control?"

"Yes."

"The Protectorate will power a super-fast mind with physical speed to match, in an indestructible werewolf body."

"Admit it sounds cool."

"I will admit that, Gavin, while also admitting the notion terrifies me more than any other aspect of our time together. Which is extremely terrifying."

"I get that. But assuming I am still evil: what do I want more than anything?"

"To go through the Wall."

"Gig, the Protectorate can't last. Getting us through the Wall is the reason it was created. It needs that focus: that journey to an impossible thing. Otherwise it will tear itself apart and we'll be back to where we were ten years ago, with wars over water in less than a decade."

The first soldier to arrive is a woman. She isn't tall, but her body is powerful, like a wrestler's. The invisibility hormone ensures I'm hidden against the bark of an oak tree as she moves past.

"Gig," Gavin says. "Please."

The soldier's helmeted head whips around. However, it's not Gavin or me she has heard but two of her nearby colleagues, who lack her panther grace.

"I don't blame you for being reluctant," Gavin says in my mind. "But before you decide, can I share something with you?"

"Yes," I say.

The wood fills with light; very different to that cast by this cloudy, indifferent morning. Beginning as a silver glow, it is formed by multiplying fractals; their esoteric structures rich with information. At the heart of it is Helen, although I sense rather than see her. She is unbroken, and full of love.

The glory eases into everything I see.

I take a deep breath, bringing in those incredible woodland smells: new branches tight with sap; the decay of older trees on their slow way into the sweet, dark soil; a beetle crunching a green leaf; the sharp stink of badgers, warm in their sett; clues to the life of the soldier before me: her just-washed uniform not quite hiding the scent of last night's lovemaking; machine oil in her rifle, talc on her neck. Further off, other lives are revealed as the decisions that brought them here become chemicals adrift in the silvery morning air.

Beyond it all: a residual trace of Becky in the cottage.

I think, 'Why would I want to leave any of this?'

"All right then, Gavin," I say, out loud this time.

The soldier turns and her eyes widen. She goes to shout, but what emerges is a low hoot; then it stops and everything around me freezes.

"Run," Gavin says. "And don't bump into anything or you'll burst like a grape under a hammer."

I dash out of the wood and through the field, where police officers and soldiers are like statues. All I hear is a continual note; it affects my balance and I stumble.

"Grape!" Gavin shrieks.

My speed has displaced the air to create a long sonic boom that sounds like the sky yawning. I clench my jaw so my lips aren't pushed open and squint against the blasting wind. This sensory confusion is too much; it's like being spun faster than I can bear.

A sudden, calculated calm expands through me as

decisions like heart rate and coordination are reallocated to the Protectorate, which uses its enormous handling capacity to ease my journey. Moving smoothly now, I flow like pale smoke through the army around the cottage. Once clear, I race away down the road into a world made bright and still for me alone.

Control

The Beanstalk Control Room is at the top of a tower in the middle of Orchard Academy. My speed and the Skywolf get me in there without anyone noticing, although I appear to materialise out of nowhere in the centre of the wide room with a bang.

After the screaming subsides, someone says, "Gig, why are you covered in blood?"

"Ah," I say. "I had to eat some cows."

There is an uncomfortable silence.

"They were beef cattle," I add, "if it's any consolation."

"But you're a vegan!" screams a man to my left.

"I appear to have lapsed," I say.

They stare at me. There are ten, none of whom I've met before. I clear my throat.

"You'll have heard some things about me," I say. "How Gavin Dergs and I are the same person; that every full moon I turn into him."

I take a deep breath.

"It's all true," I say. "Although I didn't know until a few weeks ago."

I find it hard to meet their eyes.

"I tried to kill myself," I continue, "but it's harder when you're a werewolf."

One of the men nods. The woman next to him stares.

"What the hell are you nodding for, Ranjit?" she says.

"I don't know what else to do," Ranjit says.

Another woman comes towards me from a large bank of controls. In her mid-twenties, she is of Chinese heritage, with glimmering black hair to her waist.

"My name's Li," she says. "I'm the Launch Captain."

We shake hands.

"Great title," I say.

"Thanks," she says and points to Ranjit. "He came up with it."

Ranjit waves. The woman next to him is still glaring.

"What?" he says.

She shakes her head.

"Gig, um, there's a warrant for your arrest," Li says.

"Yes," I say.

"It's authorised by the King."

"And Parliament," I say.

"Right," Li says.

I clear my throat.

"You should probably… ah…"

"Call someone?" the woman next to Ranjit says.

Li swallows, looks away and then looks at me again.

"What's that rifle?" the vegan man says.

"It's not really a rifle," I say. "It's a kind of harpoon gun with a sucker on the end that uses superstring. It's called the Skywolf."

"Awesome…" the vegan man says, his eyes huge.

"It looks like a rifle," Ranjit says.

"I suppose it does."

"And you are a seven-foot werewolf," the woman next to Ranjit says.

"Indeed," I say.

"Not much we could do," Ranjit says. "If you wanted to

get away or something."

"It's the 'something' I need help with," I say.

Everyone looks at Li.

"What would that be, Gig?" she says.

"I need to go up the Beanstalk."

There is an astonished pause, then the woman next to Ranjit gets up and comes over. It is like a signal to the others, who follow until I am surrounded.

"Why?" Li says.

"Tonight is the full moon," I say.

"Do you want to turn into Gavin and die in space?" the vegan man says.

"No," I say. "I want to go through the Wall."

They stare, and then there is an eruption of questions.

"Enough!" Li yells and there is immediate silence. "Gig, how exactly are you going to do that?"

"The Welsh Protectorate is now a hybrid human/supercomputer," I say.

The team absorbs this uncomfortable new truth.

"Thought they'd gone a bit quiet," the woman who is now standing next to Ranjit says.

"They have been working on a solution based on everything known about Gavin, everything known about me and everything we have been working on for the past ten years. Information is only part of it; we need an actual physical force, such as electricity; smart electricity if you like."

"Sounds dangerous," Li says.

I point through the window at the Beanstalk.

"The safest place to find out is up there."

"Can't more tests be done?" Li says.

"The only test is to actually do it. Tonight is our last chance."

"Would it be so bad if we… don't do it?" Ranjit says.

"We'll be fighting over water in a decade's time," I say.

"Probably less."

A couple of them nod; several appear confused and I can't tell with the rest.

"Gig," Gavin says in my mind, "we literally do not have all night."

For a moment, I feel as if I'm losing everything; their attention, Gavin's patience, time... I take a deep breath, and let the words come.

"A dire outcome like that seems inevitable," I say to the team. "Everything feels as if it's set in motion, and there are many, many variables; most of them outside our control. So we need another way: something other than catastrophe to alter our course. This could be it."

I look past the Control Room Team out of the window around the top of the circular tower. It's late afternoon on the first clear day of the year. We usually get these days after the summer when the air is cooler; however, this is June, which tends to dense humidity. Today, though, I can see past the Beanstalk to the dark steel bow of the horizon.

"Let me show you," I say.

I point at a terminal.

"May I?"

Li nods.

My access codes have been rescinded and so have Becky's, but Helen's haven't. I use them to open facility control programs and direct the Academy to link directly to the Protectorate. The Protectorate then diverts power to the Academy from all over the Kingdom and the Northern Republic. This new information connects satellites and transmitters; it also reconfigures cables to carry the Wall penetration signal to the Beanstalk.

"Er... Gig?" Li says.

"Just a moment," I say.

"No, really," Li says.

I hit the last key and turn to her.

"What's this?" she says.

There are symbols on the monitors no one in the world has seen before. They are silver, and appear to be both within and outside the screens, like a 3D display. As the symbols glow brighter, tendrils of white energy extend into the room.

"That would be the... What I was talking about," I say.

"Will it hurt us?" Li asks.

"No."

Ranjit touches one of the tendrils.

"Woh!" he shouts as the tendril breaks up into a star pattern whose limbs extend into a scatter of glowing points. "It taught me —"

His voice becomes more resonant and musical as he speaks. It sounds familiar, and I remember Becky in the temple, singing a new language into being.

Ranjit's eyes widen.

"This could work," he says.

The tendrils branch and begin to link.

Li reaches for one, hesitates and then touches it. She closes her eyes.

"Anybody who wants to leave should do so now," Li says, echoes of the new language behind her words.

Nobody moves.

"I need complete control," I say, "so no one can turn the power and data off, or bring the capsule back to Earth until I'm... er..."

They regard me for a moment; then move back to their workstations, which envelop them in strange light.

Only Li remains beside me. She opens her eyes. Their irises are silver.

"We won't see you again, will we?" she says.

"No."

Her tears contain sparkles.

"The Academy is now on lockdown," she says.

The team's musical voice gets louder. Li's hands move in the spreading light, as if she is stroking moonlit water.

"The capsule is in launch position with its external controls locked," she says. "Only you can fly it now."

"Thank you, Li."

"How are you going to get to the launch platform?" she says.

I lift the Skywolf.

"Ah. I wish I could have had a go on that."

"One day," I say.

"Yes."

My big dumb werewolf heart aches more than it did when I ran here. Li reaches up, takes my face and draws it down with her slender hands. Light bursts from our lips as they touch.

When I let go of Li, the blood that covered me has gone.

"Goodbye," she whispers.

Her eyes remain open, but she no longer sees me.

Crossing to an open window, I attach the Skywolf sucker to the floor and climb out. As I lower myself to the ground, the control room above becomes an eerie beacon, spilling silver light into the evening.

First Stage

I race across campus, everything slowing to silence around me. Fountains become water sculptures; trees resemble motionless models of themselves and people look like waxworks, complete with blank eyes and a faintly nauseating sheen to the flesh. I could be running through a photograph; there is that same desensitised feel from moving faster than the chemical reactions that create my sense of smell. Only the scalding press of air as it rushes through my fur connects me to this paused world.

Orchard Academy is ringed by a single huge building. It takes me seconds to run from the Control Room to the curve of the great structure's inner wall, and I have so much velocity I leap three storeys onto the grassy roof. I slow down, and tear a great smouldering gash in the rich green turf.

The Beanstalk is a distant gathering of filigree cords with an unmistakeable sheen, as if whatever colour you shine on them gives back only silver. Further out, the sun is low on the water and blinding gold. Between me and the waiting capsule is the perimeter fence, a forest I planted for the oxygen, and a mile of deep ocean.

I can't risk being trapped in one of the huge tunnels linking the spaceport to the Academy, so I swing down the outer balconies, jump the security barricade and run into the forest. The smells I inhaled earlier catch up with me; barbecue smoke, summer sweat and that perfume supposedly based on me that I never got any money for.

("'Unleash the wolf within'?" Helen roared when she heard about it; "That's the worst tagline I've ever heard! What's the ad going to be? The police turning up to a slaughter at some party, saying, 'What's all this about then?' and someone saying, 'Oh, Sally unleashed the wolf within'.")

The young forest is big enough for its mixed aromas to reach me before I get to the cliff on the far side. Oak and beech, some conifers so it looks green in the winter; the smell of deer and fox. Presently, the heady mix of brine and ozone herald my approach to the sea and I slow down, more carefully this time.

The ancient, dark grey face of the basalt cliff sheers down to a small cove, which is cut off from the rest of the coast even at low tide. I fix the Skywolf to an exposed section of smooth oak trunk and back off the cliff edge, playing out the superstring as I descend the heated rock to the beach.

I cross the pale sand to the sea, releasing the Skywolf as I go. The steep incline through gentle surf means I'm quickly up to my waist, the water surface a chilly tickle around my abdomen.

I aim at a leg of the spaceport platform and fire. When the sucker attaches, I lie back in the sea, my footpads facing the Beanstalk. I set the Skywolf controls to reel in as fast as possible, tighten all my muscles and pull the trigger.

I'm yanked upright; but engage Gavin's speed so I have time to get my balance right. For a second I have the weird sense of standing on water, then I ease into normal velocity and water-ski on my pads across the ocean.

I keep my hips at the same height above the surface to avoid being hauled over, although accommodating the small waves has my legs going like pistons. Water rushing beneath my pads begins to heat them as the spaceport fills the horizon. The burning quickly intensifies, but I ignore it as I do the increasing ache in my legs. I must maintain this speed; it's faster than a boat but not as fast as a torpedo, and should confuse the platform's defences long enough for me to get through them.

My heart thuds with exertion and fear, but soon I'm in the shadow of the platform, and then just under the structure itself. Detaching the Skywolf from the leg, I sink and tread water.

The buildings on the outer square of the spaceport double as barricades and their high, white walls are smooth. However, there's a crane extending out past the top of one and I fire the sucker at it. When I get a connection, I pull the trigger again and water flies off as I zip upwards.

Slowing as I reach the underside of the crane's arm, I release the Skywolf and climb down onto a factory roof. I shake the rest of the water from my fur and shoot the Skywolf at a section of the nearest Beanstalk cable about a hundred metres up. I expect the cable to quiver like a ribbon; instead the impact feels like concrete. I let the superstring tighten, then run and leap from the roof.

I soar above gigantic printing facilities that will fabricate orbital goods on demand, automated stores for raw materials and robotic factories for the manufacture of customised capsules. Slotted among them are the dish antennae of communication relays, the multi-faceted dome sensors of research stations and complex, studded aerials of media outlets whose combined job is to analyse and interpret this interface with the new frontier; to somehow tell its story.

Despite the physical order, this place feels more chaotic now Helen and Becky are gone. Partway between high-tech riot and summer festival, the spaceport below is dense with brightly-coloured movement. Bars, squares and balconies are full of people: some see me and wave as I fly over; others shout, but I'm gone before I hear them.

The huge launch pad gates are closed, so when I drop onto the boarding platform it's deserted. I head to the centre of the huge, square space and look up.

Cables rise from the platform's four corners to a height that is difficult to comprehend. The cables ought to form a cross, but their length is too great. Instead, they seem to fade into nothing as they point at what looks like a tiny, angular cloud: the great anchor that was once a silver rocket.

There is a transparent, spherical capsule slotted onto the southeast Beanstalk cable, although 'cable' is a misnomer. It's more like two separate strips beside each other: one for power and the other for data. They rise through the middle of the ten-metre-diameter capsule as if it's a bead on a necklace. Controls, utilities and storage are built around a floor-to-ceiling central 'island', which resembles a slim wardrobe with operating panels protruding either side.

I board and walk to the nearest control deck. One button activates the capsule power system, and its hum replaces the sea wind as I shut the doors. A red switch presses wheels against the cable ribbons and there's a bump as they connect. When I slam down the biggest lever, lasers in the platform fire up into concave mirrors embedded in the capsule underside.

The view changes as I rise away from the Earth, towards a Wall beyond space and time.

Secret Service

I'm two kilometres up with 99,998 to go when something behind the control deck goes bang.

This expedition was always a risk. Just because we never found the power/data resistance level of the superstring doesn't mean it isn't there. We are currently beaming the equivalent of a hundred Internets of data and enough electricity to power Britain into the anchor station. The station is then returning this combined power into the capsule via all eight sections of cable. The hope is that some sort of transformation will then occur to answer the question of who, what and why I am, thus finally ushering in a genuine twenty-first century civilisation.

Unless the capsule simply explodes.

There's another bang from behind the console. I release the access panel and open it.

"Yes, hello," Becky says.

She's curled up inside a storage locker, wearing a snug white exosuit and helmet that have kept her scent from me.

All the things I want to say to Becky blend into one noise, which goes something like: whuff?

She clambers out, gasping at the cramp in her legs, then takes off the helmet and puts it in the locker. As she closes the access panel, I see that her thick grey hair is in its tight braid again, slicked back using some sort of product with a rather nice petrochemical scent.

"I didn't want wispy hair in zero-g," she says, touching it with a gloved hand. "I'll look like a madwoman."

I go to speak, but instead get that exosuit off her and we make love, high above the Earth. I lose myself as usual: there is only Becky, as if the universe is in her rather than the other way around.

"How are you?" she says later.

I think for a moment.

"Mustn't grumble," I say.

"Good, good," she says and sits up to look past me. "Nice view."

"How high are we?"

"When you had me bent over the console, I saw on a readout we were fifty kilometres up. That was a while ago, mind."

I look down at the British Isles, spread like a map. I can see Europe in one direction, the grey Atlantic in another. When I turn back to Becky, she has the exosuit on again. Her eyes are wide as she smooths at her hair, even though it is still mirror-shiny.

"Becky, if I turn into Gavin, he may not be able to stop himself consuming you."

"He won't do that," Becky says.

"How do you know?" I say.

"Because he didn't before," she says.

That great black vault above the world's glowing edge seems less impressive now it has taken sudden residence in my heart.

"You knew?" I say. "That Gavin and I were one and the same?"

"I've always known," Becky says.

I stare at her. She swallows and carries on.

"When you first appeared, I was brought in by the Security Service to assess you, working from a sealed observation room. We had to monitor you during a full moon in case you became dangerous in your werewolf form, so of course I saw you change.

"Before we knew what was happening, Gavin had ripped through two agents and devoured them. It was... incredible. This blurred human figure in a thick scarlet mist... He hurled a table through the wall of my observation room and came in after it.

"I was too terrified to run, and then he was in my face: this awful mask of hatred that buzzed and hummed as it sprayed me with the blood of my colleagues. I had no idea why he didn't kill me, and when anaesthetic gas was pumped in it knocked us both out.

"Once I'd analysed you, I realised that the predatory aspect of you was your human form. Predators aren't just thoughtless monsters, though. Somehow, Gavin knew he needed me; that I was different. That I was not prey."

"Helen," I whisper.

"I know."

"Otis..."

"Yes..."

"Those are just the two closest to us, the two we loved most! What about the people who died because of that rubbish about the antibiotic? And everybody the fascists killed? What about the ones who were fed to Gavin?"

"The Kingdom needed a miracle, Gig. You were it."

My legs give out; I slide down the door.

"How are you the same person as the Becky I love?" I ask.

She smiles, but I don't recognise her. She could be the Queen of Saturn.

"Gavin was contained," Becky says. "He could only exist in the hyperspace chambers."

"You know about those too?"

"I helped design them."

"And the cleaning system?" I say. "The trolleys? Did you strap the victims in yourself?"

"The two from our shelter, who Gavin had requested. After that, none."

"What did you say to them?"

"They were unconscious."

Grief erupts from me in retching, hopeless sobs. Massive and draining, the physical anguish eventually exhausts itself, but leaves the source of misery in place. It feels like a sea of broken ice inside me; as hard to fathom and reason with as the God of old.

"You're worse than Gavin," I say. "He is what he is, but you made a decision."

"Yes."

I want to run, but stay kneeling on the floor and turn away from Becky instead.

The view outside is as calm as her implacable face. The horizon has begun to curve and there is a great and astonishing darkness above. The only sounds are the racket of Becky's heart, made distant by the exosuit; the quiet, steady drone of the capsule's air filtration system and the very faint, very soft rustle of wheels as they grip the Beanstalk.

"Gig…"

I haul myself upright.

"I love you," Becky says.

I feel old and out of place: a creature from folklore who has no business in the future.

"I love you," Becky says again. "Dark and light I love you."

Her words take a while to reach me.

"Him, too?" I say.

"I love you in your entirety," Becky says. "Can you love

me in mine?"

Yes, I can.

"Gavin doesn't need you any more," I say. "He will tear you apart and consume you."

Becky smiles, her eyes dazzling with heartbreak.

"I knew this was a one-way trip, my darling," she says. "What's the point of going on, without you?"

I manage to sigh; the unhappiest sound I have ever made.

"Why tell me?" I say.

"You would have found out anyway."

"How?"

"These days are full of revelations," Becky says. "Helen, Otis and…"

She takes a deep breath.

"A wolf escapes from a zoo," she says. "He crosses a field and something happens. Something from the Earth, or something from the stars. A mutation. A signal. A signal causing a mutation."

I stare at her.

"Becky, do you already know what I am?"

"A psychopathic prisoner is given an experimental drug to alter his immune system and generate a new antibiotic. It works too well, and the prisoner… changes."

"What?"

"The moon is created when a comet hits the Earth during its formation. The comet has in it a blueprint for another form of life, which blends with the fabric of our planet. This matrix develops over millennia, while life as we know it evolves on the surface. Slowly the alien rises like a plant, until one day in October ten years ago…"

"Becky, what are you saying?"

"I think I used to know the truth," Becky says, "but now I don't. It could be all those things. It could be none of them."

"Meaning?"

"We are going through the Wall, Gig."

The blinding is sudden and agony spreads with shocking speed, as if a million rusty needles plunge into me from every direction. I'm paralysed; my head is smashed in and my bones broken, then broken again. My lungs collapse and tighten; it feels like there's an anvil in my chest. I choke as my heart struggles; it seems ten times larger and I fight to breathe. This physical change triggers memories of all the others; they crash in on me and the pressure of it is a dreadful stabbing in my ears. Soon I reach a point where there is only pain, then...

I open my eyes. The capsule has stopped moving; everything is silent. My arm is no longer covered in grey fur: it's pale and fleshy, but roped with muscle. My fingers tremble; even at rest they move so fast I can barely see them.

Becky's expression is unchanged, but she inspires a hunger so powerful that saliva is a hot pour in my eager mouth.

Night & Day

I watch as Gavin lunges at Becky.

Strange light plays around us: not just from the moon, in sight now and fearsomely clear, but from the capsule itself.

Power and data have combined in the Beanstalk to become a single force. Normally an electrical current would distort the data and then short out; instead a single stream of energy has been created. It should earth into the seabed under the spaceport, or blow us up. Instead, the circuit is maintained as Gavin and I finally split apart, creating a zone whose demand increases.

The capsule begins to change. It's hard to perceive at first; then I see more stars, easing into view as if we are still on Earth at nightfall. The detail is far greater though; I can even see the spheres of light as they meet and deflect, illuminating the fabric of the void. There are more colours than I knew existed: they bloom and rush in a spectrum as long and varied as time.

I flex my hands in the seethe of information and starlight. The energies react and I weave patterns in the devastating flux. My claws extend into different realms as my fur moves in gales of new radiation like sunlight: immeasurably vast and warm.

Gavin is halfway across the space separating him from Becky, whose eyes gradually widen in terror. I leap at Gavin and hurl him against the side of the capsule. Light bursts in jagged patterns across the curved wall where his body touches it. He spins, launches himself at me and we tumble past Becky.

Unable to match our speed, she is like a statue that will shatter with a touch.

I seize Gavin and we roll around the interior of the capsule. I flick a claw across his shin; no corresponding wound opens on me, so I throw him against the central column. He bounces off and goes for Becky again.

I seize Gavin from behind and bite into his neck. He wrenches my jaws apart and slithers free, but when we confront each other again he sports one of my enormous claws and I've got a tiny human hand at the end of my arm.

Grey fur seethes over Gavin, leaving pale flesh in its wake. He grows; I get smaller and his features distort as my muzzle juts out of them like it's been driven into the back of his head. When the fanged maw parts, I feel his absurdly small mouth open in my face.

I sense that Helen is with us, as if the rarefied sunshine has taken human form, just behind me somewhere. Her golden strength pulls Gavin forward until he and I are in front of each other.

I resist.

I do not want that horror in me.

I do not want to become it.

It was in you all along, Helen seems to whisper. What is so different, now?

Gavin is a hairless little man again, shining blue in the light from Earth. His usual nasty expression is gone and there is pleading in his widened eyes. He reaches for me the way he reached for Helen, but I recoil.

Power surges to force my compliance; I fight it and push back. Sparks burst around us; the capsule creaks as if it's being stretched and lightning crackles along my fur. I smell burning;

sweat runs down Gavin and evaporates in the uncanny heat.

We stumble apart and the zone of our division hums with energy. As vapour shrouds Gavin, I prepare to fight him and my claws cut rainbows in the blazing air.

Instead, he backs off.

No, Helen whispers. This is not right.

Gavin shakes as the elemental storm tears at him. The grid of his being tries to re-establish itself as motes of light flick away his body; he is ripped apart and reformed, nerves charged with agony. He can't scream, but the groaning capsule provides a substitute; its dense material overwhelmed. His muscles rip along their length but Gavin still manages to stagger away, leaving bloody footprints that are sucked back into his breaking flesh.

He is… helping me.

He is… on my side after all.

He will… die before imposing himself.

We are separate now, so I will survive without him.

Gig, Helen whispers.

The power entering this liminal zone is not infinite; neither is the structure of the capsule and neither am I. Despite the stars that fill space with light both stark and milky, I see an end to it all, suddenly. If anything is to happen, it must happen now.

Yes, Helen whispers.

I run at Gavin and seize him. Everything whites out, and we blend into one.

The feeling is alien and yet familiar, like the first experience of sex. It is a sliding intimacy: simpler and more mysterious than imagined. A permission to be, as a complete entity: shocking, familiar; utterly delirious.

This time my awareness of him is total, and the horror is even worse than I expected. It is not just carnage and the freezing intensity of evil, but the sheer awfulness of his existence. His loneliness feels like the vacuum outside and his claustrophobia an endless compression of the soul. Yet I also feel the terrible joy of his power and intellect: the cold, predatory efficiency of him.

Of me.

Trinity

I turn to Becky, whose eyes brim with tears as she looks at me.

Behind her stretches the Solar System, every planet and asteroid clear. Their unfiltered colours are raw, their contours harsh amid unimaginable tidal forces. Instead of the neat orbital patterns I've seen in pictures, I sense a gravitational battle as the bodies we share space with react to pressures even my enhanced perception can barely comprehend. Nothing is soft, neat or pretty; everything is constantly on the point of falling apart. Only the capsule keeps us alive; this fragment of Earth we have brought with us, into an environment so extreme as to be the quintessence of terror.

Yet I can feel those colossal energies in my own blood, my own heart. I can almost hear them: a roar made from trillions of evolving symphonies. It is another ecosystem, and after tonight, we might stand a better chance out here.

The stars are so bright it's hard to see Becky's face, then I realise the illumination is in her as well; she radiates light and warmth. I didn't think she'd been affected by the battle between myselves; but it has altered her after all.

"I love you," she says, her voice resonant with every moment of her life and future.

"I know," I say.

She laughs, and the sound is like music.

At the moment of my joining I wondered if I would still feel the same about Becky, and the truth is that I do not. I love her more. It is not just the love of two beings who need to procreate; or the love of friends, or fondness earned over time. That form of love can be a defence: a retreat from mortal terror in the face of infinity. This love is the opposite; lit by every sun that ever was and will be, under the gaze of the universe.

"Are you ready?" I say.

Becky nods and I push my claws into her.

She gasps. It's the familiar Becky gasp of intense pleasure and is also the first note of a new register. I feel her potential amid energies knotted in their old configuration, and begin to rearrange them. Music comes from her open mouth; more notes and sounds than should be possible from a single human. The exosuit is shredded; the tough fabric settles around my claws and I weave it into my lover, strengthening her as she begins to change.

Her hair comes loose and writhes around her head; it is white now, but thick as a young woman's. Her body is strong again; the exhaustion and palsies are gone. Her toes point down and her arms stretch either side as her nails thicken and grow.

When they open, her eyes are silver orbs.

I pull Becky to me and sink my teeth into her neck. Her blood is full of stars, and delicious. I gulp it down and bite harder. My jaws extend past her neck and I bite into her shoulder; her thundering heart loud in my ears. She thrashes in the grip of orgasm as I slip into her and then...

We float as the capsule breaks out of the gravity well.

My claws, teeth and sex are all in Becky and still it is not enough. I bite her again, harder this time and once more her climax shudders through us. We bounce off the floor as the capsule shoots towards the anchor station, its geometry blinding in the altered light. I will bite through Becky's neck if I do it again, but I cannot stop: my jaws stretch, the muscles begin to contract –

She bites me instead. Her jaws are smaller than mine, but no less powerful. Her fur is white, and very soft; her ears delicately pointed. As her teeth enter my flesh it's like a deep itch has been scratched and I roar with pleasure that is close to agony.

Becky grips the console with her feet, bites down harder and shakes me like a rat. It is exquisite. She hurls me against the shifting wall; I ricochet and we seize each other beside a glittering wall with the blue Earth behind us. Her legs grip my waist; I enter her again and her claws plunge into my throat as we join in a storm of blood and ecstasy. Our minds touch –

Imperial College, London
Twelve years earlier

"Professor D'Olivera?"

"What?"

"It's George. Your PhD student? You told me to come and get you if you became, uh, trapped in the bathroom again."

I look at my reflection in the mirror, seething with rage about something someone said eight years, two months and six hours ago, while also being astonished afresh that at thirty-nine years old I still do not recognise or understand my face.

"I'm in a doom-loop, George."

I watch my mouth move, as if it is someone else's. The lips are full, but seem slightly distorted, as if the entire mechanism was added as an afterthought.

"Okay Professor. Is-is that painful?"

"It's a condition whereby I am so involved in an internal conflict I forget where I am," I say.

"I... Uh, Professor, can I just...?"

Turning from the mirror, I cross the bathroom, unlock the door and open it.

George is a big American boy who has the questionable fortune of being a nerd in the body of a quarterback. He was a virgin too, until he became my PhD student.

"Also," George says, "there are some men here."

"Not your God-bothering countrymen, I trust?"

"No. Spies."

My eyebrows rise as they do when I'm impressed. George smiles and blushes.

"They're using fake ID," he says. "The biometrics are very slightly off."

"I see."

We go through the lab. I start to head down to the entrance hall, but George shakes his head and places his hand very lightly on my back to guide me. It's not something he would have done before, and I'm sufficiently pleased that I don't notice we're headed for the Vice Principal's office until we get there.

"Oh," I say.

George goes to say something, and then walks away as the door opens.

A woman who is not the Vice Principal stands inside the office; my age, but sleek and hard beneath her expensive short hairstyle and tailored red pinstripe suit. She has a tension that smacks of too much responsibility and the excess caffeine she needs to deal with it. If she'd been male I'd have said heart attack in twelve years; I give her a couple more, but it will be cancer and not the sort you get over.

"Professor D'Olivera," the woman says in a soft Midlands accent. "My name is Jenna. Thanks for coming."

I roll my eyes and shove past her.

The Vice Principal is leaning his big arse against his big arse desk. He does not look pleased to see me, but then he never does. I smile at him because he dislikes that, while ignoring the four young men in jeans and cheap leather jackets who adorn the walls, making the office feel like a poorly attended gay bar.

"Rebecca," the VP says because he knows I hate that, "these people are —"

"MI5," I say and turn to Jenna. "Don't mess me about."

The VP looks surprised and tries to hide it. Jenna smiles.

"Good," she says.

"The best," I say and don't smile back.

"You need to be," Jenna says. "We need your assistance on a delicate matter."

"If it's delicate you'd better get someone else."

"No," the Jenna says. "We want you."

She is faking a kind of lust as she says that, eyes a little too wide; lips parted and slightly out of breath. They've done their research, then.

"For your shitty biometrics?" I say. "Forget it."

"Oh no," Jenna says. "Much sexier than that."

I raise my left eyebrow, the one I have greater control over.

"You'll have heard rumours about the lycanthrope," she says.

I laugh.

"You mean that cosplay guy who interfered with a fire rescue in a tower block?" I say.

"Cosplay guy," Jenna says. "I came up with that."

She looks simultaneously sad and frightened; this time she isn't putting it on.

"We still have some control over the media," she adds.

I blink.

"So…?"

"He's at a facility in Whitechapel," Jenna says. "We wondered if you'd come and… Actually, I'm going to leave it to you to decide what you come and do."

"Do you need anything, Professor?" one of the young men says.

I cross to the VP's desk, help myself to one of the

moleskin notebooks he keeps to show off with and never writes anything in, and a biro I suspect is mine anyway. I don't carry a handbag, preferring the pockets of my tweed jacket for the conveyance of sundry female items.

"Let's go," I say.

The MI5 team came by people carrier, which is disappointing. I'd hoped for a helicopter, or a four-wheel drive with blacked out windows. At least we don't have to take the Tube, although that would probably have been quicker as it's that late morning period in London when everyone assumes everyone else is having elevenses and makes a dash for it across the metropolis.

The Whitechapel facility is a nondescript building behind one of those barbed grey fences you find around electrical substations. A couple of CCTV cameras swivel in their darkened domes as we pass, the only sign of high-end security I can see. The vehicle stops in an underground car park; the young men seem to fade away and I accompany Jenna up some metal stairs to a door she opens using a swipe card. Again, I'm unimpressed; until I see the next door is solid steel and opened with a retina scan.

Jenna keeps looking at me with a weird mix of anticipation and dread. I try to ignore her, but her nerves have already burned through her limited-edition Chanel scent.

We reach a room that looks like a small office. There's a table with a phone on it, a couple of meeting room chairs and a snuffly ventilation system. I almost don't notice the wall with the window –

Jenna is slapping my cheeks with more force than required; my eyes open, but she throws a plastic cup of cold water in my face anyway. I'm out of breath and my body aches the way it does after I've had a long, multiple orgasm. I grunt and grip Jenna; who is leaning over me as I lie on my back on the floor. I go to tell her something: ease off the caffeine? Get another job? I'm not sure what, just as long as I'm speaking to another human being.

Instead I get a terrible image, as if driven into my head like a metal spike: Jenna screaming and covered in blood; her short hair slick with it in light made eerie by a strange movement I can't quite see. My words choke me as I somehow realise it won't be cancer that kills her; instead, something will rip her apart and eat her while she is still alive.

But that hasn't happened; Jenna is still here. My hands are on her arms and she is not covered in blood at all. Instead, she has an apologetic smile.

"No one's reacted like that before," she says. "Don't worry; this room is vacuum-sealed, so he can't smell or hear you, and that window is a one-way mirror. Come on, up you get."

She helps me onto a chair. I keep the window behind me, so I don't have to look through it again.

"Have you got… samples?" I manage.

"Some. They're difficult to obtain. The fur can't be cut and neither can the claws."

I nod.

"When you do," I say, my voice quiet, "can I take them to my lab?"

"We have better facilities here."

I nod again. My usual need to antagonise has gone, as if blown away.

"Do you need anything else?" Jenna says.

For a moment, I want her to stay; but the nightmare image I had of her death is already fading.

"No," I say.

She leaves.

I sit there for a moment, and then I turn around.

The large, high-ceilinged room on the other side of the window is concrete and steel, lit with bright LEDs. On the right, a middle-aged man in a tracksuit sits on a folding chair next to a pile of books. The man holds a grapple stick for collecting litter and uses it to pick up one of the books. He speaks, but I can't hear.

I find volume controls by the window and turn them up.

"…is a copy of the Holy Bible," the man says. "I'm going to pass it to you. Is that all right?"

"Yes."

Oh God, his voice…

The man tenses as he passes over the Bible. A huge, clawed hand takes the book and opens it.

"Everything… okay?" the man says.

"Fine," the occupant of the other, much larger chair says.

He smiles!

In his hands the book is tiny as he leafs through it and begins to read. He frowns. His face is so expressive I don't think he could hide what he feels, even if he wanted to.

"Not sure about this bit," he says

"Which one?"

"There's a… flood?"

"Yes."

"Nearly everybody dies."

"They do."

"Children, even?"

"It would seem so."

He reads on.

"I suppose the fish do okay," he says.

"I suppose."

"And aquatic mammals."

"Um, that is, you know… probably…"

The man in the tracksuit clears his throat.

"Okay," the man says to the werewolf. "Now I'm going to pass you another book. This one is called the Koran…"

I take out the biro, open the moleskin notebook and write:

I love you.

I have never felt anything like this before; I wasn't even sure love existed. We have not met and perhaps never will, but if we don't and you should ever read this book then I want you to know that whatever else happens I love you and will always love you.

My emotional connections have always been sensuous and, when I was older, sexual. My scientific pursuits are part of the same thing, as if I seek an elemental part of life that informs who and what we are. I have a gift for comprehending these existential blueprints, be they DNA, medicine or psychology. They are like music to me.

But music is not all sound variation organised over time. It relies on denial: a need the listener has for resolution. My work is the same; there is something missing just beyond my perception. If only I could get there!

I didn't even realise it was something I wanted, until I looked through a window in an office in Whitechapel and saw a beautiful werewolf chatting about the absurdities of... Not Christianity, because the part he commented on was before Christ: the Old Testament, which seemed to be waiting for the Son of God, even before anyone knew he was on his way.

I don't think you are the messiah, but I think you are what we need. I know you are what I need.

I have always felt alone. I told myself it didn't matter. I have done okay on my own: an attractive woman with an exceptional mind and luckily robust physicality. And yet I was an only child and my parents died when I was very young. I have relied on my strength for so long, I did not realise how much I needed another, or an Other, until I saw you.

It is more than love at first sight, for I feel I already know you. Neither is it the kind of love where I project my desire onto someone else and hope we can mould ourselves to accommodate it. Instead I think we will meet beyond this Wall that separates us. I believe together we will see things no other couple has seen and share experiences that will redefine humanity. My surety in this matter is so powerful it is an almost physical contact: a taste perhaps, or the touch of impossibly soft, impossibly strong fur.

When I first saw you it was akin to being at the heart of an explosion. It wasn't destructive though; it was life-giving. All possibility was contained and then released in an intolerable burst of energy.

These words are one expression of it; loud even to me, like a joyous shouting in my mind.

It's terrifying though; I know the terror will almost be the undoing of me, but that I will persevere. I have had a glimpse already; a sense that you are more than you seem, even though your lovely shape is warning enough.

My fear is bigger than that, though: it is almost a whole other sense, a means of engaging with our world and the worlds beyond. There is a hint of humiliation in it, but a hint for our own good, like an inoculation. We will need it in the millennia to come: that invaluable perspective.

My science beckons; the familiar structures I can manipulate for a sense of worth. But that is all theatre; I require a true connection now, perhaps in orbit somewhere, with you my secret friend.

How I have gone on! And yet I suddenly realise you will one day know these words, know them as if you wrote them yourself. I cannot wait for that day, and until then my life is yours.

Stars

Becky and I no longer tear into each other; instead, she is...
she has...

Gone.

Realisation is like the world shifting out of orbit: a sense of
wrenching horror as eternity rushes in.

But then I see a shape around me in the capsule like a
hurricane or a galaxy, multi-coloured and shot through with
gold. Becky has not left; she awaits me in a new form. I stand
at the heart of her as she swirls in glory. She is happiness
personified!

My claws move through her, making fresh patterns as she
winks out of this dimension to reappear in another. I see that
one too: an eerie realm of shifting grey light where the tiniest
part of Becky roars like a nova. Reappearing in the capsule, she
sweeps up and around the interior, wearing away at it; mixing
her power with its incredible strength.

Beyond the walls, the anchor station appears motionless,
despite our rush towards it.

I hang supine above the capsule floor, motionless in zero-
g. Becky's movement intensifies; she flickers in and out of
reality faster and faster as if the transitions give her energy. My
body flashes in the light beyond Earth as I grow: a terrific
stretching that feels like relief. Soon, Becky's mass is mine,

along with her power and…

She is me, and I am her.

I know everything she knows of this world and the others. My mind expands with her genius; oh, the brilliance of her! It is almost unbearable; no wonder she/I was so crazy! Only Gavin's kinetic intelligence comes close and even his aspect is nearly overwhelmed. I feel everything Becky has felt: her life a series of chapters that stretch back.

Helen is a powerful presence throughout; from their fights to Becky's envy of Helen's beauty; impatience with Helen's tendency to control and, beneath that, thwarted desire for Helen herself. It is a different thing to Becky's love for me: a chaotic counterpoint, a balance even.

Further still: her loneliness and orphan grief, never properly acknowledged or dealt with; the extreme sensitivity that made her life a constant fight with everything. There she is: a little girl in a room on her own, voices downstairs she does not recognise or like; her companion a tiny computer that isn't even hers but that she makes her own, the confiscation even of that over some minor thing resulting in hatred for every one of the devices until Orchard Product 5 makes it all okay.

Again and again, she returns to that overwhelming grief as she tries to justify her decisions. Through her eyes I see the two people from our shelter as she straps them into trolleys in the hyperspace chamber, her hands shaking, her vision of their sleeping faces blurred with tears of searing guilt.

I remember them: Johnny and Magda. Johnny was the youngest; in his twenties, but permanently weakened by the addiction to prescription painkillers he'd only just kicked. Magda was stronger, but always confused after a breakdown brought on by overwork. Becky hovers over them, her gaze flickering from Magda's blonde hair to Johnny's dark skin; then there is a grating sound above, and she runs.

Dark and light I love you.

I see myself as Becky sees me – God, how massive and frightful I am! Yet every time Becky looks at me she shivers with joy: from her first sight of me through the mirrored window in Whitechapel to her confused view of my fight with Gavin in the capsule. Her love does not deteriorate over all that time; it becomes even stronger as her body weakens with age.

I thought I understood love until I experienced what Becky feels for me. The realisation brings Gavin surging up and for a while we are three beings in this powerful werewolf body.

Then we become one, and turn again to the stars. They are part of the fabric of the capsule now; information coming in with light across aeons.

Tiny, glowing silver branches form around the curved inner walls. The branches reach for me and, when they touch, I can control the capsule with my mind. The branches wrap around my wrists and ankles, suspending me. My fur goes white; becomes dazzling. The branches multiply and grow, energy becoming matter that fills the capsule. My view is not diminished; indeed, I see in all directions.

Approaching the anchor station, I feel the Earth swing below. From beyond comes a press of strange matter and the richness between galaxies.

And... there is something else out there, something I can't quite see.

Operating the capsule at a molecular level, I ease it off the cable. The great ribbon cuts through the transparent sphere; I heal it at once and the spinning Earth flings me towards the moon.

Everything falls away, and I realise I am through the Wall.

Now I can perceive other civilisations, far away among the

stars. They seem familiar…

New frequencies transmit this knowledge to the Protectorate and I sense their astonishment, their comprehension and then: a moment of perfect understanding. It is a tiny, gentle force; an almost muscular response, like a widening iris.

I am with my pack at last.

At once, the event decays; too powerful even for me. I am a mortal creature after all, and it's time to go. Expending capsule energy, I create a jet in the vacuum and begin my journey home. Soon the blue planet turns beneath me, and I fire a long stream to re-enter the atmosphere.

Time ripples; I am in more than one era. The capsule breaks up and me with it, leaving a trail of data across multiple skies: a time tunnel through which the planet dumps its excess heat out into space.

I see a field in Kent; the Thera temple, Helen looking up – there and then not there as we slip into the past: a bright streak of everything, blazing with love.

Owooooo!

OWWOOOOOO

About the Author

Andrew Wallace is a novelist based in Kent, England. His work has appeared in *Vector*, *The Shadow Booth* and *We Are the Mutants*; he also blogs about science-fiction, fantasy and the creative process at www.andrewwallace.me. The first two books of Andrew's far-future Diamond Roads thriller series, *Sons of the Crystal Mind* & *The Outer Spheres*, are now available.

New from NewCon Press

Rachel Armstrong – Invisible Ecologies

Set in a near-future Venice, *Invisible Ecologies* tells the story of Po, an ambiguously gendered boy who shares an intimate connection with a nascent sentience emerging within the Po delta: the bioregion upon which the city of Venice is founded. The pair share a series of extraordinary adventures and, as Po starts school, stumble upon the Mayor's drastic plans to modernise the city and reshape the future of the lagoon and its people.

David Gullen – Shopocalypse

A Bonnie and Clyde for the Trump era, Josie and Novik embark on the ultimate roadtrip. In a near-future re-sculpted politically and geographically by climate change, they blaze a trail across the shopping malls of America in a printed intelligent car (stolen by accident), with a hundred and ninety million LSD-contaminated dollars in the trunk, buying shoes and cameras to change the world.

Kim Lakin-Smith – Bright Burning Star

Charged with crimes against the state, Kali Titian (pilot, soldier, and engineer), is sentenced to Erbärmlich prison camp, where few survive for long. Here she encounters Mohab, the Speaker's son, and uncovers two ancient energy sources, which may just bring redemption to an oppressed people. Set in a dystopian future, the author of *Cyber Circus* returns with a dazzling tale of courage against the odds and the power of hope.

Ian Creasey – The Shape of Strangers

British SF's best kept secret, Ian Creasey is one of our most prolific and successful short fiction writers, with 18 stories published in *Asimov's*, a half dozen or more in *Analog*, and appearances in a host of the major SF fiction venues. *The Shape of Strangers* showcases Ian's perceptive and inventive style of science fiction, gathering together fourteen of his finest tales, including stories that have been selected for *Year's Best* anthologies.

Lightning Source UK Ltd.
Milton Keynes UK
UKHW010143060319
338559UK00001B/40/P